I0547507

Feast of the Badger

and

Red Fang

Two *Stalk* Adventures

P. J. Hafner

Birchbark Publishing

This is a work of fiction. Names, characters, places, and incidents either are the product of the author's imagination or are used fictitiously. Any resemblance to actual persons, living or dead, events, or locales is entirely coincidental.

Publisher's Cataloging in Publication

Hafner, P. J.

Feast of the Badger and Red Fang/ P. J. Hafner

p.   cm.

ISBN-13: 978-0-615846453

1. Action / Adventure – Fiction   2. Minnesota – Fiction

I. Title

Feast of the Badger

One

Langston Bryce stepped onto the cold, snow-dusted surface of his backyard deck from the warmth of his living room. That was the last time he would see it.

He could have sworn he'd heard the sound for what it was, even through the closed back door. Pitch dark out, stars visible everywhere in the sky. Winter brought greater clarity to the twinkling constellations above, the chill overcoming the smog and enhancing starlight brilliance. Very cold out, consequently no bugs; a person could thus take time to view the heavens in peace. Mosquitoes would be buzzing all around his face by now, had it been summer. With what remained of the sprawling wetland near his house – as well as the hundreds of other new homes in this development – the insects still found ideal places to breed and flourish. But not now, not in winter. Some advantages to living in the north during January, Bryce supposed.

The breeze triggered a gentle rustling in the treetops, but other than that, silence gripped the chilled wetland. That is, except for the dull sounds of constant traffic from the freeway, about 200 yards from where he stood. The interstate was never empty of cars and trucks, but the din was buffered by the dense growth of raspberry bushes, nettles, and wiregrass, bunched up all the way from his property line to the big road. The wetland's thickness was amended by an assortment of trees, including dogwood, elm, and tamarack. It was so overgrown you could barely see any vehicle headlights from where he watched on the deck, just an occasional sparkle of light sneaking through the growth. Bryce remained on the platform for another moment, waiting. Waiting for that...that sound. There it was again, coming from the frosty brush just past the fence. He hadn't been just imagining the cry after all, although it was hard to believe.

It sounded like a baby's cry.

Bryce started to move to the stairs, about to go down and trudge across the snowy yard for a closer look. He hesitated; get a jacket and hat? Perhaps put on boots, instead of wandering around outside in slippers. Good ideas both; he was in his late 50s now, and finding it harder to stay warm like in the past. Best to bundle up and then go out; however, on TV a hotly contested NBA game was wrapping up – he couldn't miss the finale. Have to make it quick. Plus dinner was long since done, and he now craved dessert; back inside a container of spumoni ice cream seemed to call to him from the freezer.

Called to him, as did the crying voice out in the darkness. Before leaving the house he had turned on the deck's floodlight; the entire yard had become illuminated. But further ahead in the shadows, near the source of the sound, it appeared even blacker than before, as the yard light caused a contrast between bright and dark.

Did some neighbors fail to watch their toddler? Was a little kid now lost? Maybe, although by now he'd met a large percentage of the folks in the nearby houses, and young children were fairly rare in the community at this point. While pondering the thought, a gust of wind brushed across his face. The chill of it felt colder than the inside of his freezer, the one storing the ice cream he now lusted for. Get back inside, he urged himself. He stepped in and grabbed a knit cap off the coffee table there, and pulled it over his neatly groomed, silver head of hair. The cap was an old one, royal blue, and proudly displayed the logo of 3M, his company, embroidered on the front.

He stepped back out just as another gurgled moan, and a cry, sounded from the weeds and slender trees populating the rear of his property.

Uh. Uh. Waaaa.

Bryce scrambled down the stairs of the deck, then tip-toed through four-inch deep snow to the fence's gate. He opened it and stepped forward, straining to see anything in the blackness shrouding the thicket. Looking for a shape perhaps, or some movement. He could detect nothing at first, then another cry floated to him: squeaky, soft, desperate. Just 20 feet away. The noise sounded like it was coming from a child younger than a toddler, more like an infant.

Waaaa.

At the sound of the crying, protective urges welled up from the primitive sections of his brain. Bryce went forward, guarding his eyes against sharp branches amidst the brush. Stepping with care, although the slippers did little to protect his feet. Flakes of snow tumbled into the footwear and packed up against his skin, melting and forming a frigid dampness. He was certain the sound had traveled to him from a spot directly ahead; he pushed aside a handful of dogwood branches, and maneuvered his way closer. Shivers coursed through his chest and back, the beginning of his system's protection against hypothermia: just one of many ways the body tries to preserve itself. Shivering to generate heat, in order to stay alive. But for the purpose of survival, for staying alive, on this night Langston Bryce could have used more.

***

The predator waited as Bryce trudged past his hiding spot, then rose up in slow motion, matching the movement of the surrounding brush as it swayed in the breeze. The intended prey – Langston Bryce – stumbled and slipped through the snow, weeds, and branches, looking unsure, frightened, and clearly out of his element. Looking to save an imperiled child who did not exist.

The predator experienced little discomfort from the cold, even while he'd held still in ambush, swaddled as he was in garments of leather and fur. Wearing clothing of the ancients. The leather, made from deer, coyote, and cattle skin, blocked the wind; hair from the same creatures insulated the majority of his outfit. However, his face and hands were protected behind a buckskin facemask and gloves, the coverings lined with soft rabbit fur. Even cannibals need their creature comforts.

As Bryce looked ahead, straining to make out shapes in the brush, the predator's form floated to him. The killer timed his motion with whistles of the breeze to mask his footfalls in the powdered snow underfoot. Bryce continued facing away, unaware, even as the predator's club whisked in a semicircle toward his head. The weapon struck the victim's head at the temple. A killing masterpiece similar to those used by the predator's ancestors, it usually needed to connect just once in the right spot to accomplish its task. Such was the case for this attack. As the body of Bryce went limp and collapsed to the cold ground below, the club remained fixed at the spot it had struck: a 4-inch blade, fashioned from bone and honed shaving sharp, protruded from either side of the club's striking section. One side of it had lodged into Bryce's brain, turning off the lights there forever.

The primitive blade had to be yanked out so the quarry could fall completely. After doing so, the predator covered the deadly club ending with a dense leather sheath, then stuffed the weapon into the deer hide satchel slung over his back. He'd need both hands free for the next part.

As he positioned himself near the warm corpse, prepping for the big lift, the predator thought of the call. The cry of the endangered child, the forlorn infant. Hadn't used that one in a while, hadn't needed to. It still worked; always would. The predator spoke very little of the language used by the man he'd just killed, but those sounds shared a commonality. Throughout time, adults wanted to protect babies, so that call as a lure was an effective choice. He took no great joy in the deception, but as a hunter, the predator used what worked. He had to, or he'd starve.

He made the lift of Bryce's dead body. Scooping the corpse under the head and behind both knees, then hefting it up – like, well, a heavy baby – he continued the lift's momentum and in one motion flung the load over his left shoulder. After a short distance he'd switch shoulders, and continue to do so back and forth, to prevent either side from experiencing extreme exhaustion. He'd done it before with other victims, including deer much larger than this man. With solid, functional muscularity developed through a lifetime of hunting and gathering – and lifting heavy things – the initial hefting was easy for him; but the exertion wouldn't be easy a few minutes from now. He knew that from plenty of experience. Had to get going.

The predator trudged into the darkness, his victim draped over a shoulder, through the brush directly toward the interstate. Car after car and truck after truck whizzed by, all oblivious to the butchery that had just taken place right off the freeway, back in the black wetland. Forty yards from the interstate, he stepped with care into a drainage ditch, most of it filled with muddy, pungent water, still flowing despite the cold weather. It remained open year-round, thanks to countless springs endlessly bubbling up from the swamp, the warm water from the springs flowing together to form the weed-choked creek. The creek's water in some spots was knee deep, in others up to mid-thigh. The predator knew this, as he'd traveled this same dense creek since he was a child. He knew where to step, where fallen trees were at the creek's bottom, and the deeper spots to avoid. In some locations the creek was only about 12 feet wide, in others almost 25. The water was chilly, but it didn't bother him. So many previous treks through this drainage ditch had made it second nature.

The predator, still lugging his prey, inched his way down the creek just over 100 yards. He stepped to the waterway's middle, then across to the other side. He maneuvered through a cluster of tall cattails by the creek's edge, and nudged them to the side with his free arm. Keeping the body on one shoulder, he crouched toward a pile of branches on the bank. The bundle was made of the driest, lightest branches he could find, and for the purpose of concealment, the limbs had been tethered together with dry grass. He clutched them and lifted them away in an easy motion. Underneath was a hole in the mud, roughly three feet high by four feet wide. The entrance to his underground lair.

Here was the tricky part. He couldn't fail in this next step, couldn't drop the body anywhere on land, just in case the searchers used tracking dogs. Dropping the prey in the water wouldn't matter, as the scent would be washed away instantly. Hence the navigation by creek instead of by land. But the smell of the body on the shore's grass and mud would be hazardous at best. It could result in the end of his endeavors...of him.

Swinging the body around, so that the head pointed downward toward the lair's opening, he took a breath, then lunged forward. With a grunt and a burst of power, the predator managed to fling the body through the earthen opening. It traveled into the blackness, and landed below with a thud. Perfect.

The predator stayed up top for a moment, catching his breath. Looking up at the sky, he studied the stars, not unlike Langston Bryce had done recently. A couple of minutes later, the heat from the effort started to dissipate from his body; it had built up easily under the insulation of his garments. Once underground, he'd start a routine campfire, disrobe, and let the comfort return. And then some cooking and feasting would commence.

The predator stepped into the hole, nimble foot placements finding the dense tree roots that formed his stepladder. He grabbed the bundle of branches that had covered the hole just minutes ago. After maneuvering it over the top of his lair entrance for camouflage, he then disappeared into his living quarters, joining the body of Langston Bryce down below.

Two

"So this is the area where the abduction took place," said Norman Jenkins, Police Captain of Plano Lakes, Minnesota. "That third house in is Bryce's. Familiar with all the new construction around here?"

As the early morning light increased, they looked over the expanse of wetland, standing on an icy asphalt path that wandered from the cul-de-sac. A large number of recreational paths like this one had been included when the Majestic Maples housing development had been built. And like this path, the others were also covered in a deep layer of snow during winter. Just a smattering of the local residents' boot tracks appeared on them from time to time, in some cases along with those of their companion dogs. But mostly the paths remained abandoned until warmer weather arrived and the snow melted. Plowing them wasn't in the budget, not for the City of Plano Lakes nor the local homeowners association. Consequently, many snowy paths led from many cul-de-sacs dotted with many – *many* – gigantic new homes.

"Great view of the freeway from here," said Lee Bodkin, ignoring Jenkins' question. "A couple of convenient entrances to it from the frontage road. One entrance just a few blocks north of us, and another a half-mile south. Did anyone check for disturbances in the snow along the frontage road? Like drag marks? The body could have been hauled out there and thrown into a vehicle."

"My crew did a drive-by or two, didn't see anything," Jenkins said.

Bodkin looked over at Jenkins. "They tried to piece

together the scene from a patrol car?"

"It's cold out. Plus disturbances in the snow are easy to see. Anyway, I think the place to start looking, and looking hard, is across the interstate at that trailer court." On the other side of 35W, over about four city blocks' worth of wetland and one wide expanse of concrete highway, sat an aging trailer park. It was three football fields long, and consisted of inexpensive units with fading paint, deteriorating roofs, and broken windows repaired with materials such as duct tape and cardboard. Most of the trailers were 40 or 50 years old.

"Lot of drunks, druggies, assorted riff-raff come and go there. Wouldn't be a bit surprised if one or more of them got involved in a kidnapping," Jenkins said.

"Has there been a ransom demand of some kind?" Bodkin said.

"Nope," Jenkins said.

"Did Bryce have any dealings with the properties there? Know anyone there?"

"No reason to believe so."

"So there's not a revenge factor, most likely. Was Bryce's house robbed?" Bodkin said.

"Doesn't appear to have been," Jenkins said. "As you see, his house is situated back from the street just a little further than the other houses, so neighbors wouldn't have a real easy time seeing someone approaching in the dark. Even with the snow. Maybe that made his place a more likely target."

Or him.

"So no family around to provide some insight?" Bodkin said.

"No, he lived there alone. Divorced ages ago. No kids," Jenkins said

"Ask around over there yet?" Bodkin said, nodding in the direction of the trailer park.

"Nah, we don't go in there unless we have to," Jenkins said.

"Just in the case of urgent matters?"

"Pretty much, yes," Jenkins said.

"Wait around long enough and something urgent just might show up. Who knows, maybe someone will disappear from their backyard," Bodkin said.

Jenkins didn't reply, just did another once-over of Bodkin. Jenkins had heard a few of the details; the guy was a purported legend, area law enforcement's go-to when they needed a contractor. Some fed agencies too, supposedly. Jenkins wasn't impressed. This guy thought he had it all under control; but he had no police training, was just a semi-thug in earlier life, mixed it up later with a bunch of wrestling and martial arts activities. And now tracked crooks into the woods and weeds. That was apparently supposed to make him a big hero. To Jenkins, those things were just sports and outdoor adventures. Kids' stuff, really, compared to being an actual cop.

As Bodkin walked away from him a few feet, studying the wetland, the patches of forest, and the trailers across the interstate, Jenkins took another look at him. All dressed in faded garb, like a construction worker, contrasting to Jenkins' pressed, dark blue police uniform. The guy's upper legs had the enlarged look, like a sprinter's, or maybe one of those powerlifting buffoons. And his shoulders appeared to be wider than his waist. Probably just the insulated clothing, Jenkins thought. Thick neck holding up a block of a head, on which the hair had been buzzed down to sandpaper. But anyone could grow a neck like that if they lived on protein shakes or whatever.

"What would be the motivation of a trailer court resident to do that? And where would they bring him?" Bodkin said.

"Where? No idea. That's why we're hiring you. Along with that wolf mutt of yours, and your hot little partner."

Bodkin didn't at first reply with any words, just calmly looked away from the field and directly at Jenkins. He held the captain's eyes for a moment, and Jenkins cleared his throat and looked away.

"Dare you to say that to her face," Bodkin said finally, the look in his eyes switching to amusement.

"Which one," Jenkins said, in an attempt to recover.

"Either." Bodkin looked back across the field, and over at the distant trailer court. "Doesn't really seem like those types, drinkers and druggies as you say, would have the go-power or the interest to come all the way across a busy interstate to grab a homeowner from his property."

Bodkin sensed the proud captain was full of it. Didn't know where to start, so he instead threw out half-baked theories. A full-grown man's body had been removed completely from the premises. Hadn't driven or walked away; the inside of the house was intact and lived in, TV left on, used dishes not yet put away, his car still in the heated garage. Pretty much vanished into thin air. The chain of events required to make that happen had to be done with a purpose, not off-the-cuff or casually.

The physical signs in the snow showed he walked into the backyard, fell over – killed? – and his footprints then stopped. The cops with their dress shoes and spiffy uniforms had found that much. None of them ventured into the brush or deep snow, though; that task had now been set on Bodkin's plate. After he'd quoted them his fee, they wanted to make sure they got their money's worth.

According to information Bodkin had been given on the phone, it looked as though Bryce was picked up and carried away by someone else, whose track in turn simply faded away in the wetland. The police contact who called Bodkin thought it sounded like the weirdest thing; Bodkin, however, had seen much weirder at this point in his life, but didn't say so.

"It looks like tracks of different kinds wander all over the fields out there, through the thickets and so on, but we doubt any are from the perpetrator. Probably just from wild animals or neighborhood dogs. Might want to examine those," Jenkins said.

This guy, thought Bodkin. "I plan to. So what was Bryce's line of work? "

"He was – or is – some kind of director at 3M."

"What division?"

"I have no idea. But he's got a position of importance, and some of his network includes Plano Lakes city council folks. Thus the priority assigned to my department, to get out here and find out what transpired. And find out where Bryce is now, for that matter. If I were you, I'd look for clues leading across the freeway." Jenkins started to step away, then turned back. "And Bodkin? This is catch-as-catch-can. Whatever it takes to bring down any creeps involved. You can call us if you need backup."

"All this coordination for just one guy. I must say, this Langston Bryce must be pretty important."

"Well...the complete situation may involve more than one victim. We're not sure yet," Jenkins said.

The sun grew a little brighter and the breeze a little more brisk. Bodkin waited.

Jenkins continued, "A couple of younger folks have yet to be accounted for, but a crime related to their status has yet to be reconciled or concluded."

"In plain English, please, Captain Jenkins," Bodkin said.

"OK. Two missing, the first reported by parents last

November, and the other just three weeks back, by a sibling. One male, 19, one female, 21. Locals. Newly arrived locals, I mean," Jenkins said.

"By newly arrived, you mean from the massive structures they've put up behind us. The ones housing people with more money."

"That would be them, the people of Majestic Maples. More money, less caution."

"Why would they need caution?"

"Uh, well, the long-time residents tend to stay cautious. Based on some stuff that happened in the swampland many years ago, when I was just a kid. Similar to the recent disappearances, actually. From then on, the long-time locals don't go out in the weeds much. They stick to the roads, stay in their vehicles," Jenkins said.

"But newly-arrived folks may be a little less careful, in contrast," Bodkin said. "Like going out on these suburban trails here. Maybe even in the dark."

"Maybe. Basically, we don't know where the two I just mentioned exactly went on the nights they were last seen. They were reported to have been in the area, walking, but we don't know that. A friend could have picked them up and drove off. One could be living in Texas and the other in Florida right now, for all we know."

"But it wasn't confirmed that they actually moved; like packing up stuff and driving off in the family SUV," Bodkin said.

"No. Just sort of...gone. But you know younger folks," Jenkins said.

"Has it occurred to you that telling me additional details, like extra missing people, might have been helpful?"

Jenkins cleared his throat. He'd expected a more

compliant freelancer, one simply happy to get the extra work. "We'll go from where we are. And the city can't afford to have a revenue source like the Majestic Maples development dry up. We need those property taxes. Can't have folks scared off," Jenkins said. "With that in mind, I'll add: tactics outside of normal police procedure will be considered acceptable, Bodkin. Even unethical methods. From what I hear, it shouldn't be a big stretch for you."

Since meeting Jenkins, Bodkin smiled for the first time, and replied, "I'll come up with something."

"Plus, no need to bring in the scumbag or scumbags alive. I also heard you and your partner can grasp that concept," Jenkins said.

Bodkin smirked and shrugged, then turned away and looked out over the field again; Jenkins noticed he didn't confirm that last assumption, but didn't deny it either.

Three

Bodkin approached the creek, taking in its pungent smells: decaying plant matter, rotting branches, dark muck. He'd trudged for just over an hour along the path of the big prints, the ones that were apparently owned by the suspect...the abductor who'd carried off Langston Bryce. The imprints first traveled to the area by the suburban homes, then became more concentrated in the thorn patches and scrub brush – a great place to wait in ambush – then came back to where he now stood. Toward the interstate, the creek, and away from the houses.

But first the tracks snaked, clear as day and from behind, to where Bryce's tracks had plowed and tripped through the snow. Came up to the smaller tracks, then joined with them. The attack. Suggesting the attacker had floated in from behind, perhaps using the softness of the snow and the rustle of winter breeze as cover. Like Bodkin himself would do, although he preferred to end a stalk from more of a distance, and with a weapon. Typically an arrow for deer, a shotgun slug or buckshot for human targets – for those bad guys who insisted on shooting back instead of surrendering. But he'd also been forced to use bare hands or a knife on past manhunts, when he had no other choice. When that happened, to get close he'd channeled his movements into ultra-stealth mode. Similar to what the attacker looked to have done at the Bryce incident scene.

The tracks he inspected appeared to have been made by large, soft-bottomed leather shoes of some kind. Each indent in the snow resembled what you might expect if a person set down a small sack of potatoes over and over on the ground: wide, heavy, weight evenly distributed compared to a standard human footprint. No tread pattern at all, like a typical commercial boot would have left. Giant moccasins? That would be a new one.

"Sheba," Bodkin said, at a low volume and just once. The long-legged dog ahead of him in the snow responded with just that voice command, moving with calm steps back to his heel. He alternated between letting her roam and calling her back; wanted the dog to pick up any information she could, but also had to rein in her own paw prints. Otherwise the track could get altered, or even obliterated.

Amongst the signs they followed, blood drops appeared occasionally and in varying quantity. Sheba smelled each imprint, but inspected the ones accompanied by blood with greater interest, excited and curious by them. The breeze was gentle this morning, and made the blonde fur on her muscled, slender neck flutter in a lazy motion. At times the hair in the center of her back stood on end, at other times remained relaxed. She probably sensed both predator and prey, sensing the predator would defend its kill; yet the trail was not brand new, and immediate danger thus not present. She trotted without effort across the swampland, whether her feet touched on ice, frozen mud, or snow. Even while allowed to roam, every minute or two she would look over, wolfen eyes meeting with Bodkin's, looking for direction from him.

He gave none back to her; his dog might be flummoxed by the scene, but he was even more so. Why was the victim's body being carried? To abduct him while keeping him alive was the most likely possibility. But, if that was the case, why was there no ransom call to relatives yet? Keeping him captive while getting information out of him perhaps? But even if so, why cart his body, alive or dead, clear across wetlands, weeds, and brush, instead of to one of the suburban cul-de-sacs, where a van or car's trunk awaited? For some reason, the figure hauling Bryce wanted him back here, in the dense growth. Maybe to bring him then to the service road across the creek, where a vehicle would be parked? Unless he – or they – wanted to dump or bury Bryce back here for some reason. Winter didn't seem an optimal time for either, with frozen ground and slippery ice to navigate across. Was there some other reason to carry the victim back to this area, something more unspeakable maybe?

His job was such a joy; Bodkin read tons of books, on history, war strategy, survival, nomadic tribes, things like that. Plus plenty of fiction. But mostly adventure and detective fiction, no occult stuff, such as with werewolves or vampires and similar. Horror fiction. No need to, once you saw the things humans could do to other humans. Then you didn't need to read about monsters. They were already amongst us – he and his partner Gladdis had seen it firsthand too many times. Most people simply didn't realize how close to it they often were. Bounty hunters, especially his rare type who pursued culprits into the countryside, into remote cabins and river bottoms, often saw too much.

He continued along with the unusual tracking job, pausing many times, holding still and looking ahead, then to the left, then to the right. Over and over, for an hour plus. Seeking any discarded bits of clothing, or possessions. Maybe more blood. Seeing nothing additional, he'd finally made his way to the creek. It was basically a drainage ditch a mile long or so, separating the dense wetland from the frontage road and booming freeway next to it.

It wasn't long before Bodkin felt a little extra confusion regarding the trail. Some disappointment as well. The big, smooth prints stopped at the creek's edge; he'd expected that. What he didn't expect was what he saw next, or to be exact, what he didn't see. The snow walls lining the creek on the far side, some of them large drifts, others lower, caked snow barriers, were all undisturbed. Intact, and as smooth as when they'd fallen from the sky and been blown into place by the forces of nature.

Not stepped on. Not plowed through, not stomped down. Meaning...the abductor of Langston Bryce had not crossed directly from the tracks on Bodkin's side of the creek and continued on to the nearest side. Anything short of flying up and away meant the maker of the big prints had navigated the creek. In the icy water, mud, debris and all. In the middle of winter. With another adult in his arms, or across one shoulder. The victim being dead or alive didn't matter: that was a lot of weight. That burden would be heavy to carry anywhere, but doing it all the way across a field of swampy brush and into and through a squishy, cold stream was uncanny. Out of Bodkin's league even.

What possible destination could be downstream, to where an attacker would bother carrying a carcass or living body? Bodkin peered way down the drainage ditch, the equivalent of five city blocks or so. A small industrial park had been built there years ago, right on the service road. Four or five businesses at the location, nuts and bolts type places. From driving by it a few times over the years, Bodkin believed it contained a small parking lot, just enough for a few employees and some delivery trucks to pull in and maneuver around.

Small area, yes, but plenty of room for a vehicle to pull in and for a dead body to be loaded and carted away.

Possible...but plausible? Why bother doing the activity so far away from the attack site? It didn't make sense. And if Bryce had been killed, why move him at all?

This case might not be the slam-dunk Captain Jenkins had pictured and described. Some inept, drunken lowlife from the nearby trailer park wasn't a likely perpetrator in such a scenario. More like a powerful athlete...or something else. Psycho? Or worse? The same fee would apply to carry out the job, be it crafty criminal, nutcase, or fiction-style beast. No raise for lunatics or monsters. Wonderful.

Bodkin let his eyes float along the creek, first on the near side where he stood, then back and forth on the opposite side. Then down the center of the waterway. As his examination continued upstream, something made him glance back, over to a group of dead branches in the middle, just 40 feet away. He zeroed in on a bundle of fabric trapped there; looked like a little sack of some kind. Dull blue and half underwater. Staring at it for a few seconds, he realized it was a soggy winter cap, most likely cotton-polyester fabric, now stained a filthy gray from the drainage ditch water. Bodkin focused on the lettering displayed on part of the hat. An *M*, visible from a horizontal perspective, as if on its side, the rest of the cap under slushy water. Didn't mean anything to Bodkin, at least not at first. Just another piece of once-good clothing, lost or pitched, and now destroyed.

He again looked up ahead along the creek, seeking clues amongst the dense thorny brush lining the water on either side. Then it hit him. Growing up in Minnesota, he saw the logo everywhere: print ads, billboards, television spots, product labels. And sometimes on clothing of its employees, as the company's world headquarters operated here. He realized he recognized the *M* on the discarded cap. *M*, as in *3M*.

Some kind of director at 3M, Jenkins had said, when describing Bryce.

A moment later, Bodkin navigated the frigid, dark water, step by step. His high rubber boots repelled the icy water for the most part, until his left foot plunged into a squishy sinkhole on the creek bottom; that leg went into the creek to mid-thigh. Cold, filthy water rushed into the boot, drenching the sock inside.

Moisture-wicking, thought Bodkin, but not flood proof. He would have swore out loud, but what would have been the point? This was at least the 500th time in his life he'd had one foot or both drenched in cold water thick with mud, be it in creeks or swamps. If he lived long enough, he'd probably reach 1,000 muddy foot baths. He yanked the foot from the grip of the slick sludge and plodded on.

Bodkin gently maneuvered the wet cap from the tiny twigs holding it. Sure enough, once pulled from submersion, the hat's logo read *3M*. He stepped along through the debris and slippery stones of the creek back to shore. Sheba watched him return, then smelled the soggy cap in his hand as he stepped up. As she then looked up at Bodkin, he could tell the scent from the cap held her attention; in other words, it contained a familiar scent. One of the odors she'd been smelling as they tracked, almost for sure. Making it pretty certain the hat was from Langston Bryce.

His feet about to freeze after being covered in the wet filth, Bodkin decided to call it a day. This was just the initial sweep of his investigation. He examined the cap for just a second, preparing to stuff it into his jacket pocket. Just then he felt a stiff object in the fabric, like a piece of a twig. He turned the cap, intending to pinch the twig and flick it away. At the spot where the object resided inside the hat, a round hole appeared, about one inch in diameter. Bodkin noticed a darkening around it, looked like a wine stain...or similar. He knew in an instant what it was; blood had soaked into the material, retaining enough of its characteristic color despite the water of the creek. The flowage of the stream was slow and chilled, not conducive to washing away a substance as stubborn as blood. Bodkin wasn't surprised at all about the blood or the violated fabric, and he now knew what he'd expected anyway: the guy he was searching for was no longer alive. And the gaping hole made in this hat, which had covered the skull of Langston Bryce, confirmed it. Bodkin suspected it was from a bullet.

He examined the fabric for the twig thing, and found it. Much more significant than a twig, though. A slender, sharp shard of something – looked like bone – about the size of half a pencil had slid into the material. Bodkin removed it from the damaged hat. The edge of one side of the shard was ragged, as if snapped off through force. The other side looked as sharp as a fillet knife.

What the...

In the world Bodkin lived in, involving the pursuit of bad guys with weapons, and the need to become an equal or worse bad guy to defeat them, the arms you used were ideally as modern as possible. Hollow point bullets with the best-rated performance, shotguns retooled for smoother and foolproof performance; military-quality fighting knives, their blades adequate for field dressing a black bear. High-tech synthetic clothing to manage heat and chills alike. Optics for spying and night vision. Extensive testing of said gadgets. Then to compare those top-quality, modern contraptions to this. The thing that had possibly killed the victim in this given incident.

A piece of bone.

For the other half of his income, his other passion,

Bodkin made classic wooden longbows. Perfectly tuned, from wondrous wooden materials, varnished and sealed with the best methods known. But despite the classic and primitive nature of the weapons he made and sold, the bows usually were used in conjunction with modern arrows and broadheads. Made with automation, machined at a factory, constructed from stainless steel and aluminum. In contrast to this bone shard.

Like something used by cave men. Or maybe their descendants.

He looked at Sheba once more, but she had no answers. The section of bone had caught her attention. She licked her chops, revealing long, white fangs in the morning sun. Bodkin glanced once more at the piece of splintered bone, then wrapped it up in the hat and pocketed it. He then thought about what kind of person, or subhuman, might use something like it to stab another person in the head. What kind of sadist would it take? To drive a bone into someone's brain? Monstrous. There was that monster thing again.

Bodkin then concluded, in order to get a better understanding, maybe he should start reading some of that horror fiction after all.

Four

Gladdis Montrose whisked across the snowdrifts on lightweight snowshoes. The sun flashed along the bright aluminum portions of the tactical footwear, bursting back glints even brighter than the glare off the powdery white stuff. Bodkin almost kept up with her. But Montrose was the streamlined lioness to his muscled rhino, and he generated more heat and sunk his own snowshoes further into the fluff. In comparison to her, Bodkin's heavy physique slowed him just that little bit, enough for Montrose to exceed his pace. *Muscled rhino: yeah, that was it,* thought Bodkin. Oh, all right, maybe *overfed muscled rhino,* but he wasn't lagging that far behind.

"Doing OK back there?" Montrose asked him, turning her head to see. As she did, the breeze flickered a cluster of her bright blonde hair back and forth, over her face and fleece earband, then twisted it up in the air again. The chill of the wind made the already pink skin on Montrose's face a tiny bit more colorful, and caused her blue eyes to glow a little brighter. As her breath heaved upon resting, clouds of steam floated away in the frozen air.

"Of course I'm OK, just doing some extra reconnaissance. Don't want to miss any clues," Bodkin said, climbing over another crumbling snowdrift.

"Let me know if you see anything," Montrose said. Agile, petite, and deadly, she continued gliding and floating across the frozen wetland, around irregular clumps of dormant wiregrass, crispy cattails, and frozen puddles.

Sheba darted in front of Montrose, surging ahead with little effort, turning every few seconds to see where her companions were. Waiting for commands. Receiving none, the dog returned to her journey, long legs navigating snowy brush without a flaw. Bodkin watched the dog, glad she was along with them. For kinship and love, yes, but in a practical way too. Like any good working dog, this animal could detect sign like no human being would ever be able to. Although on today's outing, the ability to gather evidence hadn't yet mattered. No new evidence to find.

Not yet sure of her master's mission today, Sheba trotted along in the cold, fresh air; she looked enthused. Probably smelling rabbits, pheasants, and mice in the brush. Accounting for some of that eager look, no doubt. And the hungry look. All good, and nothing new. And even better, if the hunted criminal appeared, the dog would ramp it all up as they pursued him.

She'd have to restrain herself today, however. No prey to chase down, to outsmart, to trap or conquer. No, Sheba would have to relax and wait today. The three of them had just carried out a couple of passes along the creek, the one Bodkin had explored just yesterday. The same big tracks, made by the likely suspect, were still there and had faded little. The cold was nice in that regard. Conversely, in warm weather, such as that which arrived in March in these parts, the same snow would melt in a matter of hours.

New tracks could help round out a story and point the way. Today, though, it was the absence of tracks that was most significant. They'd went all the way down along the creek to the small industrial park on its opposite side, with its handful of manufacturing shops. As they went, Bodkin was amazed that Sheba couldn't pick up any new scents, any new directions to inspect. It appeared that the goon who carried Bryce away not only could plunge into a stream and disappear forever, he was also odor-free.

In turn, both he and Gladdis used their strengths, namely superior vision, to discern immobile objects...a rare advantage over a dog like Sheba. To enhance the viewing, they each carried and employed compact binoculars, scanning the distant spots but finding nothing useful. The only fresh tracks on the side of the creek where they stood were from lightweight animals – foxes, crows, rabbits and similar – and the far side of the creek contained smooth, undisturbed walls of snow. Nothing had left the creek and stumbled over them. Not even at the point where the industrial group's parking lot stretched to within just 35 yards of the creek. Bodkin was sure that right there would be the spot where the creep slogged out of the creek and to a vehicle, either still carrying or perhaps dragging the body of Langston Bryce. But...nope. Undisturbed snow, no sign of activity through any of it.

Now they were on to phase two of this outing. The purpose of today's activity was for investigation, but not just doing the outdoors stuff. Since the walk along the creek produced even less for them today than it did for Bodkin the day before, they'd now move on. To the primary objective of the day.

Plugging a resource for information, for answers.

Destination: the home of Albert Kane, one of the original residents of the homes which had popped up here decades back. The ones built way, way before the gargantuan homes of the Majestic Maples development had ever been a gleam in a developer's eye.

Police Captain Jenkins, in typical know-it-all form, figured the old guy might be worth talking to. The other residents weren't situated to see the vast stretch of wetland as was Kane; plus his house was on a legal wetland, the unit's permit to exist there grandfathered in from a time when the city wasn't as environmentally conscious. So his home sat there by itself, no one else within 300 yards of the property.

In addition, the Plano Lakes police department knew Albert Kane on a first-name basis: if any local punks appeared to be up to things unseemly, Kane called it in. Often with the warning that he was a gun owner – implying that things might escalate? The gun part was a fact, for sure, as Jenkins knew Kane competed with a bunch of other oldsters at the nearby trap and skeet range. Kane was a cranky 80-something with loaded guns, and in plenty of practice. Yeah, Jenkins mentioned to Bodkin, they honored his complaints...to avoid worse possibilities if they didn't.

As they trudged on the snowshoes toward Kane's place, Bodkin hoped the old guy wouldn't mistake the approach of the three of them today for troublemakers or thieves. He was too tired to dodge shotgun blasts right now.

"Appears we're in luck, Blondie. Looks like the guy's outside already," Bodkin said. He preferred that situation, being able to give the first impression of a couple out in the snow with their dog, just walking over to chat. A much better approach than law enforcement coming to his door, with their uniforms and badges, to interrogate.

"Does he have a big dog we should know about?" Montrose said.

"Captain Jenkins wasn't sure," Bodkin said. "If so, Sheba should be able to intercept when needed. She's looking pretty hungry today."

"Didn't you feed her before leaving this morning?" Montrose said.

"Yeah, but an active wolf dog can always use more protein," Bodkin said.

"What if it's something like a pitbull?"

"She loves pitbull sirloin. Let's go find out," Bodkin said.

***

As they drew closer, they could see the guy doing tasks in the snow-covered yard, a big pair of oversized, insulated rubber boots on his feet. It turned out he was clipping sections of raspberry branches, whose tentacles had wound around the yard's old wooden fence. The guy was leaning on the fence by the time they got close. He watched them, appearing void of emotion. Bodkin could see he was in fact 80 or so, maybe older; but he looked somehow youthful, giving off that stubborn aura of energy some active seniors radiate.

"Stumbling through the winter wonderland I see," said the old man.

"She trains me in these things," Bodkin said, lifting a snowshoe-clad foot.

"Try it in plain boots some time," the man said. "Not so easy."

"Been there," Bodkin said, shaking his head with a knowing expression. Acting the simple bumpkin, a familiar role he used from time to time. Lee Bodkin, the affable, easy-going small-town guy. Which he wasn't. "I hope we've not been stomping through your property here," Bodkin said, gesturing directly behind them at the field.

"Nope, that's state land. Plus, the two of you didn't appear to be hooligans. Well, not her anyway," said the man, sharing a quick grin with Montrose.

Bodkin stepped forward, taking off a glove and offering his hand to the other man. "Lee Bodkin," he said. "And this is my partner and quality control expert

Gladdis Montrose."

The man offered his hand and a nod to both. "Albert Kane," he said. "Haven't had such quality control in my life for almost 11 years now."

Bodkin and Montrose waited.

"My wife died about a decade ago, is what I meant," said Kane.

"Sorry to hear that," Bodkin said.

"Don't be. You have your own problems," Kane said. He smiled a little more fully. "As partners, you probably know what I mean already."

"Um, well, we're not like a husband and wife type of thing," Bodkin said.

"Thank God," Montrose said.

Kane continued smiling, gazing back at her.

"You didn't pair up based on looks, I can see that," Kane said.

"What's that supposed to mean?" Bodkin said, reaching his hand up to examine one side of his face. Theatrics. The 195-pound brute with the tender ego.

"Bring your handbag and vanity mirror next time," Montrose said to Bodkin. Turning to Kane, she said, "Albert, have a minute for a few questions?"

Kane paused. "You part of the police effort that's suddenly started over there?" he said, looking north of his plot, over to the massive Majestic Maples development.

"Yeah, we're helping out," Bodkin said.

"So you'd like to chat. If that means inside, over coffee, then sure," Kane said. "You imbibe?"

"His bloodstream is 25% espresso," Montrose said.

"Excellent," Kane said. "No espresso machine here, but I can brew it dark and mean."

"Ah, yes. Love some motor oil," Bodkin said. They walked to the side door of the house, with Sheba stepping along, but hanging back just a little. Evaluating. Bodkin stroked her head twice, saying, "Be a good girl, and wait here. If he's harming us inside, I'll yell, and you leap through the window."

The dog just looked at him, amber eyes relaxed and unimpressed.

"In a heroic rescue. This will be your chance to shine."

Sheba still stared at him, still waiting for a comment that was actually witty. Bodkin turned from her judgmental evaluation, and followed the other two inside.

The interior of Kane's two bedroom, one bath house was plain, rustic, and functional. And clean. No used dishes on the counter, no dust bunnies, no cobwebs. Just a couple of tiny smears of mud on the floor, by an entryway rug placed in front of the kitchen sink. Hey, Bodkin thought, nobody's perfect.

"So you can really move on those snow hoppers," Kane said to Montrose, who was now sitting at Kane's kitchen table, next to Bodkin.

"They help. I'm a little better on Nordic skis, actually," Montrose said.

Kane fiddled at the coffee maker, sprinkling Columbian grounds into the filter, adding some cold water, and clicking *Start*.

"Great way to stay in shape," Kane said.

"Yeah, that's a nice by-product; I actually compete on them," Montrose said.

"While she shoots a rifle," Bodkin said. "Such skills. I have a hard time keeping up."

"A rifle with skis? So you're a biathlete," Kane said. "Impressive."

"The times when I win the contest it is," Montrose said. "Gotta get a little faster."

"And of course hit what you aim at," Kane said. Montrose didn't reply, but looked pleased.

"She always hits what she aims at," Bodkin said.

"Wow. So the two of you are some kind of sharpshooting duo, then," Kane said.

"No, she's the deadeye here. I prefer to get up close," Bodkin said.

"Get close enough, hard to screw it up," Kane said.

"That's the idea. So, Albert, sounds like you've seen all the scurrying around at the new development, with cops pulled up next to each other chatting for long periods and such."

"You bet. Even witnessed some negotiating and trading of donuts, looked like from here," Kane said.

"I like this guy," Bodkin said to Montrose. "Anyway, Albert, you've seen the cops looking around, talking to people, or at least to each other. Maybe a politician or two wandering around networking with the neighborhood folks, being the important voters that the residents are. But we don't care too much about that. Gladdis and I are assigned to the more, let's say, nonstandard possibilities."

"Thus the arctic adventurer approach, like today," Kane said.

"I guess you could say that. Getting in the thick of things is sometimes the best approach. Especially since the focus of the investigation – an important executive with clout – was taken right off his own property," Bodkin said. "Disappearing, quite literally, into the thick of things."

"Or he was crafty and flew the coop. Maybe just up and left. Under the radar, for whatever reason," Kane said. "Cops are famous for overreacting."

"Oh, he was taken. I verified it," Bodkin said.

Kane didn't respond at first; to Bodkin it appeared

he was thinking things through.

"That misplaced guy must have clout, as you say. Think of all the crimes throughout the county, in this city alone; yet half the police force seems focused on this," Kane said finally.

"I thought the same thing. But the police mentioned that there may in fact be more than one person who's disappeared."

Kane paused again, this time looking uneasy. "I didn't realize that. How many others are missing? Or 'may in fact be,' as you say? Maybe they also just left."

Albert Kane, the Doubting Thomas. Neither Bodkin nor his partner had considered Kane a possible suspect. They were here largely because Jenkins had said the guy watched everything, and Bodkin saw that Kane's house was situated for excellent, long-distance wetland surveillance. Thus, he could be a great person to finagle information from. Yet, here was Kane, wanting to raise doubts as to the actual occurrence of any crimes. Maybe just an ornery bastard? Or something else?

Bodkin in turn pretended not to notice, suddenly extra interested in his coffee cup and the table. If something was being hidden here, Bodkin preferred to not tip Kane off to his own thoughts, instead just let him go on. Let him reveal things on accident, perchance. Montrose continued to look at Kane, a peaceful impression on her face, watching his eyes. She could hide a suspicious mind better than Bodkin, and her look could sometimes soothe other people, both men and women. Bodkin's look more often made people jumpy and eager to run away.

"Two others are reported missing, Albert. Whether they snuck away or not is yet to be determined. Although that's unlikely at this point, the police department informs me," Bodkin said. "The focus is on the executive who vanished, in any event."

"Big surprise," Kane said.

"That's how it usually works. Big shots go to the front of the line. So...assuming someone came to the home of the abducted individual to grab him, they probably scoped things out first."

"That would be the logical thing to do," Kane said.

"So perhaps you saw something, or somebody, out of place," Bodkin said. "That's what we're hoping for today. To give us direction. Anyone appear on the side roads, parked or on foot?"

"No one out of place, no," Kane said. He took a pull from his steaming coffee mug.

"How about out in the field, or way over by the frontage road?"

"Sorry," Kane said.

"And I figure nobody was sneaking through your yard, heading to the new houses on the ridge," Bodkin said.

"If people had, I probably would have shot them," Kane said.

So I heard, thought Bodkin, though he said nothing.

"Lee's asking these things because we were told you kind of watch over the area. Over the neighborhood," Montrose said. "Sort of like the good shepherd." She then smiled.

"*Bah.* Good shepherd? You don't know me," Kane said. "I care only about myself and a handful of friends I have left. Retired long ago from First Systems Grain, over on Highway 117. Worked in that warehouse for a long time, forklifting, some supervising, more forklifting. Stayed close over the years to several folks who also weathered their time at the company. There are three of us left; I see them about once a month, at the Yellow Perch Pub. You know it?"

Montrose nodded, and Bodkin replied, "Drive by it now and then."

"You should go in some time. The few of us get together and have a couple of beers, or two or three shots of gin. That's all I can handle nowadays. Other than those fellas, I see some other guys and gals, all younger than me, when I shoot clay pigeons. I'm in a league. Shoot twice a month, except in winter. Those are the only people I talk to. For the most part."

"Better than nothing," Bodkin said.

"True, but my point is, I'm not a good citizen. No shepherd to the neighborhood. The watchful eye for the local people, the original local people, was around here once, but is now long gone," Kane said. Then he remained silent, looking at the other two.

"We're all ears," Bodkin said "Please continue."

"That sentinel, a guardian, watched over a proud people. For millennia, and in this very area near the end. The guardian is now gone, physically, but still in the area in spirit."

"Who were these proud people, to borrow your phrase?" Montrose said.

"A Native American tribe known as the Kasa."

"Never heard of them."

"Look it up. The Minnesota Historical Society has it all documented. Plus, thanks to my parents, I have a memento from their tribe. Genuine. Come and take a look," Kane said, rising from his chair. He walked slow but steady into the living room. Montrose followed seconds later, and Bodkin, after slamming down the last of his dense coffee, did the same.

Bodkin was composing another few questions, aiming to ask them of Kane then get out of here, when his mind redirected from the inquiry to the weapon on the wall. Kane stood before it, examining it and gesturing to Gladdis. Saying how his parents were societal researchers back in the day or something.

It was a spear. Didn't appear to be a curio, nor a simple souvenir either. The weapon looked like a functional piece, once used for utility, now retired. Not a toy.

Bodkin stepped closer to the wall in Kane's living room, as Kane said a few more words to Gladdis, then turned to him and spoke. Bodkin didn't listen, but still nodded to Kane as if he was. He flickered his eyes back to the spear, sitting in its display rack on the wall. Some feathers and decorative dried weeds and dehydrated flowers adorned the display as well, but Bodkin couldn't have cared less about them.

Search, rescue, seek, and destroy were all specialties of his, but craftsmanship like that before him was as well. A lengthy shaft, about six feet or so, formed the bulk of the tool. Bodkin made longbows for half of his living, and he thus knew woodwork. The spear's shaft material didn't register with him at first, as it wasn't one of the types that he used for cultivating bows. But finally he recognized it, after another 20 seconds of Kane's blathering and history lecture, none of which he heard. Walnut. Black walnut. A hardcore wood for a very serious weapon. Comparatively rare, sturdy, and difficult to work with. But once done, a tool made from walnut was solid. Almost rock solid. For primitive people, it would be analogous to titanium. A weapons maker and material geek such as himself could have savored the moment and the workmanship of the spear shaft, it's perfection, sanding, smooth sculpting, and glazing in one type of sap glue concoction or another, ensuring its longevity against the elements. Bodkin could have, would have, if here alone. And if the head on the spear hadn't transfixed him.

Bright yellow-white, almost nine inches long, the blade on the tip of the spear encouraged wonder but issued dread at the same time. One glance and Bodkin knew it was as sharp as a razor. It had tiny serrations along its edge, but otherwise the surface had been sanded to eliminate any nicks, bumps, or slivers. Smooth as silk, in order to penetrate and kill like the caress of the grim reaper.

"Bone," Bodkin said, half to himself.

"Yes it is. Helped along with stone grinders to make the sharpest of edges. That's like a big bone butcher knife at the end. Ouch," said Kane. "Very old. To say it's an antique is an understatement."

"Ancient?"

"Certainly is," Kane said. Then he turned away. "Lady Gladdis, let me get you that refill," Kane said to Montrose, taking the coffee mug from her hand and moving to the kitchen with mincing little steps.

For a moment Montrose took in the spear tip herself, then glanced at Bodkin, sensing the weapon lust and intrigue now flowing through him. She didn't share it, but appreciated it. He glanced back, taking in her relaxed and knowing expression, face and eyes almost as beautiful to Bodkin as the spearhead before them. He gave a third of a smile, then took one last look at the prehistoric weapon. She left, joining Kane in the kitchen.

Bodkin reached up in order to brush his fingers against the bone blade, inspect the blade in a tactile way. He withdrew his hand then, started to turn, and felt the slightest of twinge in his index fingertip. Looking down, he realized a miniscule slice had opened there, a small blood droplet already forming.

The incision had occurred with next to no pressure. Barely a touch. What if the thing came flying from 20 feet away, thrown with full force by a skilled hunter?

Bodkin knew the answer, after 15 years of bowhunting deer and bear, harvesting them with stainless steel arrowheads. A blade of that quality would make a complete pass-through, slicing most everything in its path, often even bones. Vital organs would be destroyed without hesitation. To a non-hunter this might sound repulsive, but to a hunter, especially a primitive one, the effectiveness of a weapon could mean the difference between life and death, starving or eating. Bodkin put his hand with the micro cut on it deep in his pants pocket; it would bleed for a minute, then heal in short order, like any tiny cut made from a sharp edge. Sharp, like a razor.

Bodkin walked into the kitchen, and accepted a refill of his coffee mug. With his intact hand.

"So the guardian's spirit still soars above the area, but physically, he's long gone," Bodkin said.

"Yes, gone in that sense. The presence is much weaker now, but will never leave these wetlands," Kane replied.

"This spine-tingling legend have a name?" Bodkin asked.

"Yep. They called him Hone."

"Hone? That's it? Not very catchy."

"That's it," Kane said. "His name was simple, but his reality was not. The name Hone caused the enemy to tremble. Ornery pioneers, thieves, or enemy native tribes, it didn't matter. Trust me. They'd think twice about coming out into the wetland and assaulting the Kasa, once they learned about Hone."

Five

"The cops just said, 'What do you want us to do? We aren't all-seeing. We aren't big brother.'" Tina Babbitt leaned back in the armchair, on the edge of crying. But not quite. Until her sister was found, dead or alive, she wouldn't know for sure. There was still hope, she believed. No body, no crime. Nice phrase, thought Bodkin, but trite. Simple and easy to say, as if a body couldn't be made to go missing. Permanently.

"They didn't even come out?" Gladdis Montrose asked. She had shed the hunting clothes from the outings earlier in the week, and was decked in a shiny black leather jacket, rayon slacks, silk blouse, and boots with a heel. Bodkin, sitting next to her on Babbitt's couch, was dressed with a similar approach, as if going to a trendy restaurant. No beat up, swampland manhunt stuff. Montrose had inspected him when picking him up, and only directed him to change the pants. He came back out with nice wool ones on, his only pair, from his only suit. With a dressy dark shirt untucked and polished brown shoes, also meant to go with his suit getup, he looked presentable enough to meet with an upper crust suburbanite. Long, charcoal grey camel coat, also his only dressy one. Masquerading as sophisticated.

"No, they had me come in to talk," Babbitt said.

"You're kidding," Bodkin said.

"No, I wish I were. They told me that over the phone," Babbitt said. "So I went to the station. Made no difference though."

Her sadness created a stark contrast to the house's grandeur, its elegance. Adjusted and decorated to perfection. Welcoming, suggesting a feeling of cheerfulness. So much space, for just one person. Not long ago, it had housed two.

"Anyway, thank you, Mr. Bodkin, for contacting me. I'm more than glad to talk about Francine, and what she normally did, places she went," Babbitt said. "Our parents are both gone now. There's been no one else to talk with regarding her situation."

"Any neighbors come over to chat and offer condolences?" Montrose said. *Maybe reveal any knowledge of the disappearance?*

"Uh, that would be a no. A neighborhood like this, nobody really talks to each other. I've tried a couple of times with the people on either side, and the ones right across the street. They're polite, but no mutual interest, I'm afraid," Babbitt said.

Suburbia. And Bodkin thought living out in the swampland, where his simple rambler sat a few miles from here, was lonely.

"I should mention, I do appreciate your sympathies, both of you. But Francine and I weren't close. Ten years apart, and she was trouble to my folks for a long time. Lots of drugs, running away," Babbitt said. "I was in college, then grad school. I basically was no help at all. But as Francine started getting her act together lately, I offered to let her move in. Make up for lost time, I guess. She was starting a small business; making a little money too."

"Good for her. What kind of business?" Bodkin said.

"Beads. Those decorative, new age bead accessories. Bracelets, necklaces, that kind of thing. She herself wore beads, lots of them; sold them for a living, mostly on e-bay, but also at festivals. Both online and in her peer group she was known as the Bright-eyed Beadster. She was always a gentle soul, and cheery once sober. The artistic lifestyle suits her."

The three of them were quiet for a moment. "The last time you ever saw her, what were the circumstances?" Montrose asked finally. "Did she say she was heading out?"

"Well, the fact is that I had a late-night business dealing. A client was in town, and my team at the firm took them out to dinner after a long day. In downtown Minneapolis. By the time that was done and I came home, it was almost midnight. She was gone. I have no idea where."

"I assume no kind of note had been left or anything," Bodkin said.

"No, we weren't like that. I was a landlord to her more than I was a sister. But at times she would wander out in the dark, just stroll and dream up stuff for her art projects. When the county built the paved paths through the wetland, she took to them. Trying to embrace nature as she wandered, I guess. A break from her beloved computer."

Reprieve from technology and confinement. Perhaps taking a walk in the dark for escape, only to end up right in the waiting clutches of a predator. Life is grand.

"Her car wasn't missing, correct?"

"She didn't own one, but my spare car, a Civic she was free to use, was still parked in the garage."

"No friend or partner she would have rolled off with?"

"There was no partner. Her friends down in the city knew nothing, and hadn't seen her for awhile before then anyway."

Bodkin and Montrose waited.

"It's not looking good, is it?" Babbitt said.

"I'd be lying if I said it was," Bodkin said.

"Even if she's gone – I mean, as in dead – it would be better to know about it. Than to wonder and twist in the wind forever," Babbitt said. "You never know though. She may turn up. Her life has been a whirlwind the last few years; she's done some weird things. Who knows, a week from now, she may be sitting with me here again."

Hope springs eternal, thought Bodkin, but there wasn't much hope here. The day before, the two of them had visited the house of the other missing youngster, 19-year-old Loren Ware. Similar story: a disjointed relationship with roommates, in Loren's case his parents. He, like Francine, was a wanderer. Just roaming out to escape, to light up a joint possibly, his dad had confided. Into the dark wetland? Both folks thought that as good a possibility as anything else. They had been transfixed, however, by their usual three hours of TV that night, and never knew he was missing until the next evening. Loren worked at a local burrito restaurant part-time, and was usually still in bed when his parents left for work. They didn't know one way or another if he was in his room when they'd departed that morning.

Now Loren Ware, like Francine Babbitt, had vanished. Circumstances similar to that of each other, it appeared, as well as to those of Langston Bryce's disappearance.

From the police report, Francine was approximately the size of her sister Tina. About 5'4". Langston Bryce was reported to be of medium build, but stood 6' 1". An attacker who could pick up – and carry – a guy the size of Bryce, would find a woman the size of Ms. Babbitt here to be child's play in a struggle.

It wasn't about a fair fight. With serial killers, which this was starting to look like, it rarely was.

Francine Babbitt, 21. A druggie and wayward child during junior high, becoming a budding entrepreneur, straightening out her act, starting to make money. Had kicked the addictions. To end up...where? Going by Tina's statements, very little chance existed that she left town on her own. Francine's sister Tina, caring as best she could while trying to make up for lost time, with a sibling she barely knew, was hoping against hope. Tina hadn't seen the things he and Gladdis had, Bodkin knew. Hadn't seen the vermin of their fellow humankind feeding upon the vulnerable. The helpless.

So many things about this blossoming situation were unclear, but considering the mounting evidence, one thing was almost certain.

Like Loren Ware and Langston Bryce, Francine Babbitt was gone for good.

Six

Grace Dowling scraped the metal shovel across the ice, the material grating on the ice rink's surface like nails dragged across a chalkboard. Another scoop of snow and ice chips, another toss over the hockey boards. The piles of snow were forming a solid wall on the other side; soon they wouldn't even need the wooden barrier to complete their backyard hockey rink. At three feet and climbing, the snow walls would be enough.

The little brat should be out here helping, Dowling thought; his rink, his sport. But he'd just finished practice an hour ago; let him rest a little. Her 11-year-old, Justin, was the only child of she and her husband, Sean. The kid was in the hockey circuit in full force now. Not even five nights a week at the Plano Lakes Arena were quite enough for him; on weekends the mighty mite had to put in more drills, more shots on goal. Couldn't fall behind the other kids, her son had said. Dowling had told him to not be silly, but inside she appreciated it. Thought it almost necessary, even, if he ever wanted to play in the games. The other twerps were so hardcore, so specialized. Thus, she was out here now, after work and this evening's practice. In the cold, clearing the rink, getting it ready. Sean had cleared it the last two times, so now she was up. Saturday would be here before you know it, and Justin would want to be out here.

Dowling leaned on the shovel a moment, catching her breath, watching the steam from her breath float away. Looking toward the house, she tried to spy on Justin and Sean, a small opportunity to be a harmless voyeur, but the floodlight from the deck burned brightly into her eyes. She looked away from the light, toward the

darkness of the surrounding area, out toward the dense
wetland. She'd be in soon enough, and planned to make
her husband and son feel guilty, with their lounging in
front of the TV as she lumbered in all frozen.

That was when she heard it. Some kind of call from
the dark. Sounded kind of like...crying. Crying? The
thickets contained some freaky wildlife, no doubt.
Possums, raccoons, weasels, big owls that grabbed
rabbits at night. She'd heard sounds, lots of them, but
never one like just now. The cry floated to her again; a
sound of need, of mourning. As a chill went through her
– one not from the weather – Dowling decided to call
this project out here a night. Finish shoveling tomorrow.

For a third time, a wail drifted her way. That
anchored her: the sound was from a person, no question,
sounded like a little kid. A distressed kid, an infant even.

"Hello? Where are you?" Dowling said, toward the
thicket. No answer. Anything beyond the floodlight's
glow was invisible, pure black night. "I can help."

Waaaaa.

Dowling looked back once more toward the house,
but she didn't have time to go in and discuss this issue.
Not if someone's little child had wandered away. She
strained to see any motion, but while standing within the
ring of artificial light, making anything out was
impossible. She stepped forward, to the spot on the rink
where the floodlight didn't reach. To where the thickness
of the dark began.

***

The next morning, less than two hours after sunrise,
Gladdis Montrose stood on the Dowling family ice rink.
Now she had her holster on, the .40-caliber pistol it held
stuffed with 15 hollow-point bullets. A spare magazine

was attached to her belt, good for another barrage if needed. It might be. She and Bodkin had stupidly rolled without guns on their recent wetland inspections, just a sharp knife each and their charisma to protect them. Oh, and of course, Sheba. Still, not enough. Had to stack the odds; guns helped. Not many specialists in the manhunt game believed in fair fights. Most of those who did were already dead.

It had become apparent the beast was still amongst them. Possibly even watched from hiding as she and Bodkin traipsed in clueless fashion through the snow piles and brush. Most likely knew they were there, yet the carnage continued. The scumbag was close...real close.

She inspected more spots on the rink, in case anything beyond the obvious could be found. Sheba was doing the same, wandering the rink's perimeter, taking in scents. Even if nothing more was found, it didn't seem necessary. What had happened here was clear as day.

Grace Dowling had disappeared, but the mystery involved only these questions: by whom did she get taken, and where was her final destination. It didn't involve what happened here on the backyard hockey rink. No mystery. The events which had transpired were easy to see.

Big, wide tracks, similar to what Lee had shown her in the Bryce situation, had approached in what appeared to be a stalk. Not wearing modern winter boots, definitely not hiking boots. Expansive and flat, width halfway to snowshoes; impressions made by something smooth, probably a wide leather sole. Squashed into the snow by footwear that was definitely...primitive. Dowling's tracks had stepped across the rink to the edge of it, against the boards. The big tracks had left the surrounding snow and then appeared on the hockey rink, next to, and then joining, Dowling's, as she appeared to be fleeing. The assailant probably leapt the boards. Athletic attacker, thought Montrose.

Grace Dowling's flight didn't last long. A spray of blood drops marked where she fell. Not profuse though; this was no neck wound. Not a stab in the heart either. Both would have allowed much more crimson to flow, and with brighter, oxygenated blood. Probably a brain wound...some kind of stab in the head, like that suggested by the damage done to the hat Lee had found in the drainage ditch. Jesus Christ.

Montrose turned back to the Dowling house, seeing her partner walking through the snow on over to her. Bodkin looked pissed.

"The city's crack team of cops sticking it to him?" Montrose asked.

"The geniuses that they are, yes. A Mr. Sean Dowling apparently came out as his wife was shoveling snow off the family rink, killed her, and carried her back into the weeds."

"I'm sure. Why didn't they just follow the prints in the snow? Clear to see, even standing here. I'm betting the tracks never come back this way. And if they don't, then what did Mr. Dowling do to get back to the house? Parachute?"

"That would be a better guess than they're making. I almost know for certain what lies ahead here. We're going to track these cumbersome prints through the thorns, the brush, across the frozen puddles, and to the creek way over there. Where the footprints will enter the creek, and we'll never see them again," Bodkin said.

"Like with Bryce."

"Uh-huh."

"So they wouldn't let you talk to Sean Dowling?"

"No. They think he may endanger my safety," Bodkin said.

"Being the homicidal maniac he is," Montrose said.

They stared out toward the brush and swampland, beginning to set themselves for another trudge through it, figuring the end results to be predictable. But evidence of some kind could be found on the way, either dropped or dripped, you never know.

That's when Sheba showed a sudden, and intense, interest in one of the few remaining snowdrifts. The one on the side of the rink where the tracks suggested the skirmish, about six feet from both sets of tracks. She started to stick her nose in the drift, pulled back out and looked at Bodkin, then sniffed at the spot again. The hair on the center of the dog's back stood on end. Bodkin and Montrose had been letting her satellite and do her thing, but as usual, partially ignoring her.

Sheba had their attention now. Bodkin stepped to the dog, stroked her along the side once, then nudged her away. "C'mon girl. Let me take a look," Bodkin said. Sheba stepped away, then watched the spot on the drift she'd just inspected. Couldn't let her disrupt any evidence. Although any to be found wouldn't be likely in an undisturbed pile of snow. Or would it?

Upon closer inspection, the snowdrift wasn't completely undisturbed. It was pristine, except for one little crescent shaped indent. Something had passed – sliced – a little wound in the shiny snow surface, about five inches in length. Never in a million years would either Bodkin or Montrose, despite their hypervigilance, have noticed the small mark. Nor cared. But with Sheba keying in on it, it meant the mark in the snow could signify something. Hmm.

Bodkin slithered a gloved hand down into the snow where the mark lied, moving with a gentle motion, waiting for any object to be felt in the path. Sure enough, his fingers detected something other than snow, down in the snow pile no more than the width of his hand. He clamped it lightly with two fingers, and lifted the object from the drift. Montrose stepped closer to see.

Bone. A curved length, several inches long. One side splintered, as if sheared off a larger piece. The other side contained a serrated edge; it looked like a finish one of the tools in a professional butcher's arsenal might hold. A tool needed for slicing through matter tougher than red meat, like tendons and gristle. Bodkin had seen similar edges, like those on the teeth of many sharks, and in museums and books, where the daggers and slicers of prehistoric peoples were on display.

Were they starting to see a pattern here? A bone splinter here, similar to the one in the soggy fabric of Langston Bryce's hat. Only this one was much bigger than the one discovered in the creek. Actually a substantial piece from a larger tool, probably a blade. Big enough to be a blade itself. A weapon made from bone. If so, they'd encountered a bone weapon here, one in the creek...and one in another place recently. In the house of an old man.

What had broken this thing off? Bodkin looked around, and Montrose saw what the idea was here. She did the same. Hockey nets had been set up on either side of the rink; a spare hockey stick was in the snow outside the rink, nearer to the house. Accompanying those were some other objects near the rink, like a pair of sleds the family had left out, a plastic utility bucket, some poles from a volleyball net leaning against a snow-covered picnic table. Just junk not brought into the house or garage yet. Lots of people lived that way, Bodkin included.

The significance, it turned out, was that the household items served as camouflage until now. Helping to make the other "weapon" involved blend in:

a snow shovel. It was buried almost to the hilt in a corner snow pile. At first it had seemed like just another object, and they'd looked past it. No tracks were near it, but fresh powder had burst up and sprinkled new flakes across the top of the drift. It would mean nothing to a person not from snow country. Nor would it to people who were but who didn't observe the outdoors. However, to winter trackers like Bodkin and Montrose, the shovel buried like it was figured into the scene. Had to have been thrust into the drift within the last 24 hours, based on the fresh spray of flakes. Thus, possibly involved in the Grace Dowling situation.

It had to have been thrown. The closest tracks were about 14 feet away. Thrown, or maybe shot from a catapult, based on how deep it was buried. Like by someone very strong and very angry.

Bodkin stepped to the shovel, removing it from its position stuffed deep into the snow pile. Holding the tool up to look it over, it was obvious the shovel had seen some action, and not just from shoveling snow. Montrose let her eyes travel along the metal head of the shovel, then met Bodkin's eyes. He raised his eyebrows, and she responded with a slow headshake. Wowed.

The head of the shovel was aluminum, granted, but it had met its match. A wedge seven inches long had been sheared into the material, the metal pushed out on the other side like a small pair of ocean waves. Tiny slivers of something yellowish were wedged into the creases of the shovel's damaged area.

"One guess what the slivers are made of," Bodkin said.

"Looks like our bad guy had his feelings hurt when his bone blade met modern shovel. Took the shovel and whipped it."

"Yep, appears to have sent it like a rocket. I'm pretty

sure this is no slender, frail assailant we're dealing with here," Bodkin said.

Montrose looked at the attacker's exit trail, just heavy wide, smooth tracks; no sign of Grace Dowling, other than a few blood drops on the snow and some branches. Then just the big tracks. She was probably carried away, her entire body fully supported on the killer's shoulders. "I would concur with that thought. I think we've got a burly creep on our hands," she said.

Grace Dowling had apparently blocked an initial chop of one primitive, heavy axe, or something close to it. Heavy enough and sharp enough to cleave through aluminum. Then her luck ran out.

Bodkin looked at the sharp, curved bone shard one more time. He then put it in a side pocket of his Carhartt jacket – with the jacket's thick, dense fabric to protect him from the serrated edge – and zipped the pocket shut.

"Bone blades. They keep recurring in this chain of events. I think we need to drop in for another sit-down with the local amateur historian. Mr. Albert Kane."

Seven

Finally at the key spot in the tunnel, where it traveled under the freeway's shoulder, Hone attached his spear to the extension staff. The spear was just over six feet long, the staff a few inches longer yet. The end of the spear fit into the larger receptacle opening of the staff. Once it was seated there, Hone twisted the spear to snug it into threading he'd carved into both the spear's base and the staff's interior. Just that connection was probably enough to hold, but Hone wrapped a leather strap around the connection anyway, fashioning a tight knot with his wide, thick hands.

Reinforcement; didn't want the spear coming detached and dropping back down onto him while engaged in his current task. With the spearhead's deadly edge, such an event would be a hazardous occurrence. Bad enough ice chunks would be tumbling down as he worked; he didn't need something sharper coming along with them.

Just last night, the massive, thunderous people carriers, sooty discharge coming out of horns at their top, had rumbled through after yesterday's storm, pushing waves of snow off the big stone path nearby, the path built before he was born. The one that thousands and thousands of other people carriers, small, medium, and huge, burst back and forth on. Hone had felt the vibrations from them while in his lair his entire life. He no longer noticed.

But when one of the giant rumblers came through lifting and pushing snow from the big stone path, Hone had to take note, then take action. Mounds of snow, along with boulders of ice, would be pushed from the big path to the side. Hone understood the concept, appreciated it really, that the outsider pale humans were grooming their path. Just as he did in his tunnel system. Had to, as roofs and walls shifted and deteriorated on occasion. Needed to groom things, to adjust and repair them.

But when the giant rumblers did their grooming, the portals for his smoke discharge got blocked. They had to be cleared immediately, to let the smoke from his fire drift out, and wisp away into the air. Through all seven exit ports.

Long ago, before he was here on earth at all, the elders recognized the need to conceal themselves. It was no longer just an enemy tribe stalking through, or a settler poking his nose around to see what the tribe was doing, to take what they had. The outsiders, the pale humans mostly, were coming in force. More and more of them. With all sorts of people carriers, noise makers, and garden-grooming beasts that they rode on. The Kasa tribe, his people, decided to stay hidden when possible. Down in the tunnels, that objective was easy. Except for the smoke coming from their fires and drifting out up top. The smoke had to be hidden.

The big stone path aided in this effort perfectly. The people carriers bounced and rolled up and down the path at all times, emitting their own foul-smelling smoke. The elders of his tribe soon saw the solution: blend their own smoke with that of the people carriers. Blend it, but still keep it hidden.

The logical way to do this was to expel smoke in small amounts, insignificant enough to be unnoticeable. Expel the smoke through multiple exits. Right next to the big stone path, the smoke from the people carriers helping to camouflage their own discharge.

They had built seven portals, with one main tunnel

leading to them all. Hone was in the main tunnel now, comfortably wide and just high enough; he peered up at the first portal, only the slightest glimpse of sunlight able to shine through. The hole was, as predicted, clogged with snowy ice chunks.

No smoke was accumulating, however. Hone had extinguished his single cooking and warming fire as soon as he heard the giant rumbler clearing the snow. The tunnel system would quickly fill with smoke otherwise. By putting out the fire, the air had thus remained pure. But on the other hand, in return for not suffocating, Hone was starting to freeze. Tougher and more resourceful than most outsiders could even imagine, Hone was still human. The tunnels eliminated breeze, and the temps didn't drop as much down here. But when it dipped to below zero on the surface, even his best fur garments wouldn't let him survive forever. He had to move about the tunnels, to get outside and retrieve seeds and other forage, then grind and prepare them. Had to hunt, had to butcher and cook his kill. Had to get water from the creek, to drink and to clean himself. Needed to retrieve more wood at nighttime, being forced in recent times to range further and further to find any of the fuel.

And now, to make it all work, he needed to clear these smoke portals. Hone reached the tool way up, nearly 12 feet, and poked the spear at the outer edges first, and waited until sprinkles of snow came down. Then, with the cutting-sharp head of the bone blade, he wedged a stab quickly into the center of the blockage, withdrawing the blade as he jumped back from the portal. The tiny avalanche of ice crashed to the cold mud floor. Hone waited a few seconds, peered back into the earthen chimney, then reamed the hole out completely. Once it was fully open, an opening nine-inches in diameter gaped unimpeded, ready to let smoke pass by.

Hone moved to the next clogged portal.

Less than an hour later, all seven vents were cleared, the chilled air of the tunnel now being drawn up to an even more icy outside atmosphere. Hone could hear the people carriers much more clearly now. The carriers holding outsiders, strangers, but beings of little consequence to Hone.

As opposed to the new outsiders, the invading people, the ones hiding in their massive, mountain-like huts across the wetland. They'd pushed aside and ruined his land, his brush, his plants. His trees. Soon they'd overtake his water, maybe even cave in his tunnel systems. They'd kill him too, if he let them.

He wouldn't let them. His body, face, and hands felt cold now, but his thoughts let him generate a special warmth. He let his imagination roam back to the kills he'd already made, taking a few of the intruders, the thieves, so easily. Consuming most of them, giving him spiritual power, yes, but also letting him stay alive. There was so little left to eat now.

Now, but there'd be more for him soon. Like there used to be. The plants, the roots, the little fish in the creek. Once he finished off and nourished himself further with the new intruders. He'd immediately seen that they had no idea how to fight back.

Like the teachings of the ancients proclaimed: you survive by killing – and consuming – the evil ones. Until they're all gone. He'd do that. He planned to do it again, this very night.

Eight

"Of course of I've heard of them," said Lanky Burroughs. "The Kasa people were sort of legendary for their simplicity. And for their isolation."

The sun was just starting to shine with intensity through the windows of Lanky's Cafe, but only four seats remained empty. Blue collar intensity at breakfast, on an industrial stretch of freeway. Lanky rarely suffered a shortage of customers.

Lanky Burroughs was the only black man in the restaurant, just as Gladdis Montrose was the only female customer. The cafe swarmed with guys from a tool and die outfit, a plumbing supply manufacturer, an industrial brake maker, and a fishing boat factory, among other occupations. Most of the workers earned plenty, ate too much, and spent money like water. Lanky loved them for it.

Legend had it that Lanky had been an accomplished blues guitarist and crooner, based on his smooth, deep voice, his ethnicity, and his love of blues music. It was all bunk. He didn't even know how to play an instrument, much less play in a band. He happily kept the rumor going though, piping blues music with low volume and top-notch speakers at all times in his cafe. The customers thought it reminded Lanky of the more swanky and exotic times of his music tours, his legendary career. But he actually played the tunes because he, the customers, and the employees enjoyed it. No blues star of yesteryear was he.

Lanky, now in his 80s and long-since retired, had instead been a master machinist and wood mill operator, and had worked in the Boysenberry Lake Mill for most of his earning years. Earning as an employee, that is; as the proprietor of Lanky's Cafe he made more than he ever did in the mill. And he'd started it simply as an outlet to avoid isolation after retirement. The cafe's food quality never wavered, and he made more money now, and worried more about cash flow and profits, than he ever did when he cut it close financially. Even octogenarians can get greedy. But more than money, Lanky loved to gab, and even more so, loved to exchange gossip.

He placed a large dish in front of Gladdis Montrose, then turned back to the grill. The omellette in front of her, glistening with butter and infused with both sun-dried tomatoes and green peppers, wafted sweet nothings over to Bodkin. Jealousy started to well within him, but Bodkin restrained it. He knew he was next. Sure enough, just two minutes later, another platter arrived. Bodkin's omellette was equally copious, his containing shredded beef and curried onions.

Ahh, that was more like it. A typical serving here, both massive and healthy. Good for you even if you ate all of it in one sitting, Bodkin assured himself. Only wholesome food had ever been offered at Lanky's...for the most part. Until lately. A food problem, for Bodkin at least, had recently arisen.

To bolster profits, the shrewd Lanky had now introduced bakery items as add-ons. Gooey, sugar-coated, creme-filled, and cinnamon-encrusted. Dammit.

Bodkin eyed today's decadence, a tray of caramel rolls, covered with a crystal-clear glass housing. Perfectly presented, within easy reach of the customer finishing a huge breakfast, the ornate glass cover making the bakery look somehow even more tempting. Lanky aimed to have every tray of fattening bakery goods sold out by day's end. They usually did.

Bodkin today was leaning towards helping out. "How many calories do you estimate those rolls have, Lanky?" Bodkin asked.

"Forget it, Lee," Montrose said. "You're gonna pass on the extra stuff."

"Under whose decree?" Bodkin said.

"You don't remember?"

Bodkin paused, then said, "Um, mine?"

"Precisely. I was supposed to let you have it if I caught you. Per your request; I'm just following through," Montrose said.

"But...these are extenuating circumstances. We're expending massive energy on a grueling manhunt here."

Montrose pointed her fork at Bodkin's omellette mountain. "Eat," she said. Then to Lanky, "So, you were saying the Kasa people were isolated, kind of secretive."

"Sure were. Probably why almost no one's ever heard of them," Lanky said.

"Ever see any of them yourself?" Bodkin said, his eyes suddenly happier. His first mouthful of egg and curry seasoning tasted like a dream.

"Just from a distance. When I was a young guy, went over that way now and then. Highway 117 was just starting to pick up with stores and bars. Before suburbia took off over there, that was the city for us country folk."

"Beat going down all the way into St. Paul or Minneapolis, I bet," Bodkin said.

"Yep. Although gas was a lot cheaper then; we didn't know what we had. Anyway, from County Road 3 you could slow down and look over. At times the Kasa tribe members would be out in the field and the swamp, harvesting things."

"Things they grew?" Montrose asked.

"Uh-huh, and wild stuff too," Lanky said. "Cattail

roots, different seeds I guess, wild mustard for spice."

"Both organic and local," Montrose said.

"They should have opened a shop," Bodkin said.

"Huh." Lanky smiled at that. "Do it over by the prestigious Majestic Maples sprawl, you'd have suburbanites flocking in."

"Eager to show they're the most serene," Bodkin said. "So where'd the Kasa go?"

"Away, sadly," Lanky said. "And I don't mean like nomads."

"So they perished."

"That's right, to the best of anyone's knowledge. My old friend, Walt Bergen, talked about it in years past. He's a retired professor, taught down at Winona State. History. Explained to me how new people crowded into the area as the county became more and more populated. I saw that part myself, of course. Some of the Kasa had fallen ill, apparently. Then many disappeared. After that, all of them. Local air and water got tainted, over time. And almost certainly, new bacteria and viruses had crept into their lives."

"Likely new and dangerous ones. Throughout history, that's been a common problem when strange cultures meet and start living together," Bodkin said. "Sometimes a new strain of the flu is all it takes."

"Oh yeah. The flu can kill just like any other disease. Not even the tribe's guardians could save them from something as sneaky as a virus."

"The tribe's guardians, you say. We heard a vague mention of that recently. Elaborate," Montrose said.

"Well. They were the watchers, protectors, and weapons experts of the Kasa. Every peaceful culture needs someone like that," Lanky said. "Nobody ever, ever laid eyes on those guys, so it may be all just stories. But, marauders rarely bothered the Kasa over the centuries, the stories go."

Bodkin chewed with ravenous enthusiasm, Montrose with efficiency; they both looked at Lanky as they did it, waiting.

"Walt Bergen even used the expression, 'Those that stole the Kasa's lunch, became their lunch.' A statement like that sticks with you," Lanky said.

"Thieves got thrashed?" Bodkin asked.

"Got eaten," Lanky said.

Bodkin sat in silence, waiting for the punch line. Montrose also looked on, waiting for Lanky to continue.

"Uh, yeah, you mean like, literally chopped up and ingested?" Bodkin said.

"So go the tales. I was too busy working in the mill; heck, finishing high school when lots of this stuff supposedly went down. But, Bergen claims that, without a doubt, the Kasa tribe's guardians were cannibals."

Silence for a minute, Bodkin and Montrose both slicing their egg concoctions with renewed interest, and thinking.

Cannibals.

"I'll be right back," Montrose finally said, stepping away toward the ladies room. Bodkin started to come out of his reverie, the funk of weirdness involving thoughts of cannibals. He glanced at Montrose walking away, and when her small, agile form disappeared around the corner, it occurred to him. The opportune moment had come.

"Quick," Bodkin said to Lanky, while pointing at the caramel roll. Lanky looked toward the ladies room; the coast was clear. He seized a caramel roll from under the glass, flipped it onto a plate, and set it in front of Bodkin.

"Knife please," Bodkin said, and accepted a slender steak knife from Lanky's hand. One diagonal cut, and the roll was in two. Bodkin withdrew three napkins from the closest holder, wrapped one half of the confection in it, and pocketed the bundle in his jacket. The other half he started to chew with urgency.

Montrose appeared four minutes later, and Bodkin was finished with the caramel concoction. Almost all of it, that is.

Lanky went on, discussing the Kasa. "Food sources were crushed and plowed under; developers destroyed raspberry fields, cattail ponds, and entire honey locust stands. They also cut off and redirected the underground river, which had for thousands of years brought schools of sunfish and perch through to the nearby pond network. Disease might have been a final straw, but malnourishment surely figured into the Kasa's demise."

"And I suppose the new wave of people wiped out their teepees or wigwams, whatever they lived in," Bodkin said. It seemed that Montrose was not listening to Lanky at this point, instead looking over at him.

"Lee, you really don't pay attention to local history, do you?" Lanky said. Bodkin shrugged.

"They lived underground. In tunnels," Lanky said. *Underground.*

With that statement, Bodkin nearly went into an altered state of consciousness. He faintly realized Lanky was saying more, some things about prehistoric immune systems and diseases borne by new arrivals. Bodkin barely caught it. He looked down at his plate, his fork, seeing nothing, calculating recent events at a thousand miles an hour.

Bodkin was churning through Lanky's statements, analyzing, when he felt the feminine caress along his cheek. Montrose had reached up from her position next to him, running a dainty but strong pair of fingers along Bodkin's cheek, to the corner of his mouth. He felt a physical rush, and with her being his long-time partner, didn't like it but still did. Couldn't decide. Then she held the two fingers up so he could see, and she looked at Lanky as she did it.

A tiny bit of caramel residue rested on the fingertips. Busted.

Dammit. Again. Then his thoughts went back to Lanky's statements.

Tunnels. Cannibals.

Another minute passed.

"Mr. Bodkin here has fallen silent," Lanky said to Montrose.

"He's adding up his calories," Montrose offered.

Underground. One nagging question may have just been answered. Why hadn't it occurred to him earlier? Plus something else was gnawing at the back of his mind.

"He's brooding about getting caught wearing the caramel smear. C'mon Lee, nobody's perfect," Montrose said.

It clicked.

Nobody's perfect. After seeing a smear.

Just a couple of tiny smears of mud on the floor, by an entryway rug placed in front of the kitchen sink. Bodkin remembered thinking, *Hey, nobody's perfect.*

Mud. Like mud from underground. Mud from a clay and dirt tunnel. The telltale mud streak where it didn't quite fit, on the kitchen floor in Albert Kane's otherwise spotless house. By a rug that had been set there, seemingly out of place.

Plus a spear, one bearing an impressive, deadly-looking bone tip. The craftsmanship of the spearhead's edges looking strikingly similar to the two bone remnants he'd uncovered in their investigation. Just happened to be from similar bone-crafted weapons? A coincidence beyond all likelihood.

Speaking of craftsmanship: Mr. Kane stated that the

spear had been handed down to him from his folks. His folks, the societal researchers. The spear was historic; to say it was an antique was an understatement, according to Albert Kane. When asked if the weapon was ancient, the old boy replied that it most certainly was.

Bzzz! Bad answer, Kane. If Bodkin knew anything, he knew woodworking. He made half of his income slicing, assembling, testing, and finishing wooden longbows. From raw wood. He knew finishing touches, and he knew varnishes and lacquers.

The spear had been treated with a unique type of sealant, Bodkin couldn't tell what. Some kind of tree sap concoction. Bodkin had admired that substance, the sealing process used, and the ingenuity in the making of the lacquer itself. But it had bothered him at the time, despite his captivation with the primitive spear, that Kane was lying.

The spear's construction, based on the appearance and aging of the wood, was about a year old, two at the very most. When a work made from raw wood has just been finished, it has a freshness, has signs of its former life still in it. Leaning toward green wood, basically. The sealant itself will show similar traits. When old, especially a work of wood classified as ancient, the sealant is fully absorbed, sunken into the material. And the wood comes to look petrified. Beautiful in its aged state, but never to be mistaken for an object freshly constructed.

Kane's spear had been freshly constructed.

Why the lie? Bodkin at first figured the obvious: Kane wanted to impress them. Simple enough, even if lame. But now...it was looking like Kane may have wanted to conceal more. Much more.

"I hope the hearty breakfast nourished you, my adorable blonde friend," Bodkin said to Montrose. "There might be a little more action today than originally planned."

"You've got me curious, Mr. Caramel Roll," Montrose said.

"I just called you 'adorable' and 'blonde,' and you call me 'caramel roll'?" Bodkin asked.

"Preemptive strike. That's what you'll look like if you keep sneaking those extras. So what's in the works?" Montrose asked.

"Among other things, another rendezvous with the pleasant and gracious Albert Kane."

"Thought we were heading over there tomorrow."

"Change of plans. A couple of pieces to this puzzle have just fallen into place."

"Oh? What's our course of action?" Montrose asked.

"Three stops. The third one might be for keeps." With that comment, Montrose let the humorous attitude take a rest. "For keeps" meant show time.

Bodkin continued. "We have to check something out before we visit the old man. And before that, we need to swing by my place."

"Forget something?"

"Yeah. A fur-covered meat grinder named Sheba. We're going to need her."

They rose to leave. "Lanky, would I be able to fit another caramel roll on my tab? To go," Bodkin said.

"What about..." Lanky said, pointing the spatula in his hand at Montrose.

"These are urgent conditions," Bodkin said. "Extra energy may be required." As Lanky packaged up another 900-calorie roll, Bodkin took the moment to feel pleased with his own dramatic performance. Upon taking the roll from Lanky, he yet again smelled a waft of the sugary caramel. He smiled inside.

Nine

Albert Kane saw the headlights advancing up the driveway, the beams moving with frantic twitches as the vehicle bumped along on the uneven dirt surface. He stood up from the table and his freshly steeping mint tea. They'd come unannounced, and he wasn't sure what to do or how to prepare for the visit. Kane figured there was only one reason Bodkin and his partner would be returning now, at this time, fully an hour after nightfall. He stole a glance at the Persian rug in the center of the kitchen, the rug covering the trap door leading to the tribe's tunnel system. Then he looked away and down at the floor. He waited. A gentle knock sounded at the door a few seconds later.

Kane opened it and locked eyes with Lee Bodkin, who leaned against the doorjamb with his right shoulder. His right arm wasn't visible, purposely kept out of sight. Kane thought he knew why, and he was right.

"Can we come in to talk, Albert?"

"If I say no?" Kane said.

"We'll come in one way or another," Bodkin said.

Kane stepped back, and gestured for Bodkin to enter. Bodkin glanced at each of Kane's hands, which were empty, then came in. A 12-gauge shotgun with a pistol grip dangled from Bodkin's hand; it had a short barrel, just 18 inches, shorter than typically used for hunting – at least not for hunting game animals. Gladdis Montrose entered next, an insulated Carhartt outfit snugged around both upper and lower body, similar to the one Bodkin had on; her jacket was unzipped, and a polyester holster holding a flat black pistol showed at her waist. The holster's safety band was unsnapped, the pistol ready to be drawn. She looked at Kane with a neutral gaze, then let her alert blue eyes wander the room, sizing up the situation.

"Pardon me regarding the boom stick," Bodkin said, lifting the shotgun a couple of inches. "I know you're a gun owner, and I didn't want to let tonight's chat get off on the wrong foot."

"Why would it get off on the wrong foot? What do you mean, exactly?" asked Kane. In response to his question, both Montrose and Bodkin stayed quiet; they just looked back at him. Neither thought Kane appeared very surprised to see them show up like this. Conversely, he looked like he'd been discovered, caught in a lie. He lowered himself down on a kitchen chair, steadying himself on the table as he did it. Kane looked tired, more so than when they'd first met him.

"Showing up with a weapon in your hand doesn't exactly seem like police procedure," Kane said.

"We're not the police," Montrose said.

Bodkin tossed a small object onto the table in front of Kane, for a moment the clatter of it the only sound in the room. It was the shard of bone, the one found in the snowdrift along the Dowlings' ice rink.

"This what you mean by 'Hone'?" asked Bodkin. "Is 'Hone' actually his Indian name...or a name you gave him? A nickname standing for 'hone,' as in sharpen? Like to sharpen to a razor's edge. Like the piece of bony blade there."

Kane just looked at Bodkin a moment, saying nothing, then glanced at Montrose. Examining their faces, as if guessing how much they knew. Wondering how to play his hand?

"The cutting edge of that thing kind of resembles the slicing end of that 'decorative' spear you have on the wall in your living room. If I remember correctly, the bone blades are pretty similar. Or exact, possibly," Bodkin said.

"First off," said Kane, "This is not some wild west situation here in this house with me. I'm not your enemy, regardless of what you might think. That rifle," he said, nodding to an old, slender long arm, looked like a .22, in the corner near the door. "I've used it for nearly 50 years. At all times, it stands there in the corner, 12 bullets in its magazine. I can hit roofing nail heads with it from 20 yards. As targets they're a lot smaller than either of your hearts. I saw you coming, could have started popping shots before you even got to the door. Could've killed you."

"Or died trying, of course," Bodkin said.

"Of course," replied Kane. "But I didn't try, and don't want to. I'm still trying to sort all of this out myself."

"I think instead of –" Bodkin started to say.

"Shut up and sit down," said Kane. "You young punks got it all figured out, don't you, confident in your youth. Let's talk, maybe you'll learn something. Might help as you try to prevent the situation from worsening."

Bodkin and Montrose looked at each other, Montrose nodded, and then moved to the living room, keeping one hand on the pistol butt. She flipped on the light switch, just inside the room, then peered around the corner. Bodkin did the same in a back room, then went across the living room to Kane's bedroom. He examined it briefly while Montrose glanced in the bathroom. Kane endured the invasion quietly, waiting at the table with his tea. He sensed complaining wouldn't matter to these two.

The house cleared, Bodkin and Montrose came back and sat down with him, and Kane continued. "To address your question: It has nothing to do with the sharpening of weapons. Hone's the name given to him. And he's not simply a legend."

"So he's real then," Bodkin said, pretty much knowing the answer already.

"Yes, flesh and blood," Kane said. "You two want coffee?"

"We've got a thermos of espresso in the truck, but thanks for asking. Did you know this maniac was grabbing people?" said Bodkin.

"I deeply hoped that it wasn't happening. It had been so long since anything like it had," Kane said, then looked down and kept quiet.

Bodkin prompted him. "Is this phantom actually eating the people?"

"Almost certainly. In a way, it would be...tradition," Kane said.

"Explain," Montrose said. If it matched up with what Lanky had said, it was bad. Yes, very bad. People hunted down as prey. For food.

"Let's back up and begin with the section of bone here," Kane said, looking at the piece of blade on the table. "Yes, the spearhead on that weapon in the living room sports the same type of point. Bone, fashioned to a cutting tip in a very exacting way; the tribe used every bone type available. Coincidentally, both the spearhead and this shard are from deer bone."

"You've seen the chopper this Hone guy uses?" asked Bodkin.

"Countless times, although when he's brought it here, the blade end is generally wrapped in a leather covering. For the same reason you wouldn't want to tote an unsheathed butcher knife against your skin. He always carries his club. He showed me the bone blades just one time."

"So he does visit you. I suspected that, based on the

mud smears near the sink. I think you have a trapdoor there. Makes sense, since we now know his people traditionally lived in tunnels. Good guess he does too, to this day. A few more pieces of information helped it all fall into place," Bodkin said. "Surprised you're still in one piece, with his stopping by and all."

"We just trade things; it's not like some big, dangerous interaction. Mostly he brings prepared wild game; sometimes dehydrated seeds for cooking. At other times he's brought traditional curios," Kane said.

"For instance that spear," Bodkin said. "The varnish is too new, as is the wood. It's not ancient, as you told us. That little piece of bullshit you fed me prompted me to consider this situation, and you, further. Just thought you might want to know."

Kane appraised Bodkin for a second. "Touché, Mr. Bodkin. You're spot on. That weapon was given to me by Hone himself. I traded him for a box of tea and several bags of rice. Dried lentils too."

"What kind of wild game?" Bodkin said.

"Often rabbit or pheasant portions. Sometimes if we're both lucky, he's killed a deer."

"Prepared how?" Bodkin said.

"Smoked and seasoned."

"Seasoned with what?"

"One of a number of natural herbs from the fields, like wild mustard. There are dozens of them. Makes a glaze with some of the sap from the few remaining maple trees in his area."

"He's got good taste there, I'll give him that," Bodkin said, and meant it. He did similar with some of his own game kills.

"What's he look like?" Montrose asked.

"You'll know him when you see him," Kane said. "Doesn't look like today's typical, fully-evolved man.

Kind of a throwback, physically."

"Throwback, like a Neanderthal or similar?" Bodkin said.

"I guess. Whatever you want to call it, the attributes worked well for the Honani warriors over the centuries," Kane said.

"You know where his cave is?"

"Yes I do. Nearly a mile from here, across the wetland. By the interstate."

"He show you? Been a guest there?"

"A guest? Heavens no," said Kane. "I know where he habitually gathers the few remaining seeds and berries in the warm weather; I watched and followed him from a distance once, keeping in the brush as much as possible. In the summer time, when my dark clothes helped hide me. If he knew that I knew, he'd probably consider killing me."

"Oh please," Bodkin said. He scoffed, and glanced at Montrose. She kept focused on Kane, watching for any sudden movements. They weren't sure yet of his loyalty to the Hone character, and hadn't frisked him. Plus, his loaded rifle was just 11 feet away, albeit an old bolt-action. Some may snicker at a bolt-action as a dangerous tool, but Montrose herself could pound five shots through her own match-grade bolt-action rifle in three seconds, tops, working the bolt as fast as a hummingbird's wings. Who knew how good this old codger was? Best not to find out the hard way.

"Don't mistake our relationship, Lee. He's the closest thing I have left to family, granted. But he's not the son I never had. He's not a little brother. He sees me as his only human contact – only human interaction – on earth. But he keeps his distance. I'm not considered one of his tribe. Never have been."

"So what the hell is so appealing about this goblin to

you? What's the bond?" asked Bodkin.

"*Goblin*. Good one. Not far from the truth. Say, I've not eaten dinner yet. Before I ramble on further, can I get you folks a snack of some kind?" Kane said.

"Stop stalling, Albert."

"All right. I did bring home a bag of apple fritters earlier, though. I've got four left," Kane said.

"Listen, Albert –" started Bodkin, then the specific food registered in his head. Apple fritters? "Well, uh," Bodkin said, looking at Montrose.

"Snap out of it, Lee," Montrose said, now in scolding mode.

"Um, yes, we'll pass. Please continue," Bodkin said.

"Anyway. This house was built by my parents; both professors down at the university, she an archeologist, he a paleontologist. Know the difference?"

"I don't care," Bodkin replied.

"Nor I," Montrose said. "I know the difference but don't want to discuss it."

"OK, fine. Got it," said Kane, looking down at folded hands. "So, they built the house here. Not by accident, however."

"Next you'll tell me they met Hone and decided to stay," Bodkin said.

"Met his parents, actually. And the handful of tribal members still living around here at the time," Kane said. "My folks figured they had to save them, be close by to help the last of the Kasa people survive. They built this house at the very end of the Kasa's tunnel system." They waited as Kane took a sip from his teacup.

"In any event, they couldn't save the Kasa. Disease did most of them in. Primitive medicines, like a special paste made from fermented walnuts, white acorns, and honey locust seeds were no longer possible. Not once developers cut down almost every tree in sight. The crews also plowed under the majority of edible plants. All for a couple of industrial park strips and a smattering of houses. And that was before this new Majestic Maples development came to be; the ridge where those huge houses now reside was a massive stand of aspen and oak, along with of course the maples; raspberries surrounded the trees. Now it's covered with McMansions and over-fertilized lawns."

"Progress," Bodkin said with sarcasm, shaking his head slightly. "So all of the Kasa are now gone?"

"All but Hone."

"But the tunnels remain," Bodkin said.

"They do," Kane said.

"As I said, I noticed mud specks and smears near that big rug by the sink there, the first time we visited. The rest of the house is spotless, in contrast. Seemed out of place, but I didn't make the connection until recently," Bodkin said. "Plus, he couldn't very well walk down the street to get here over the years without being spotted."

"Definitely not," Kane said, looking as if he was imagining the vision of Hone. Didn't look like real happy thoughts.

"Speaking of being spotted, if this tribe existed and flourished as you say, why didn't anyone else ever pay attention to them? Nobody watched them in the fields or by the creek?"

"Oh, they did. They most certainly did. The Kasa were assumed by locals to be just dirty homeless people living out in the weeds and wetland. No one other than the tribe ever knew about the tunnel system. The locals – the original ones who moved here before the wealthy yuppies, I mean – concluded the tribe members were simply drunken bums. Oddballs. Which is pretty funny when you think about it," said Kane.

"How so?" Bodkin said.

"The poor locals themselves are basically a bunch of blue collar bumpkins living out in the woods and swamps," said Kane.

"That actually describes me," Bodkin said.

"Er, uh, I apologize," Kane said.

"No need," Montrose said with a smirk aimed at Bodkin. "It's accurate."

"So...nobody else ever got to know the Kasa people? Seems like here or there someone would have talked to the tribe. Or did they just steer clear?" Bodkin said.

"The latter, almost without exception," Kane said. "Except, long ago, when I was young enough to still be working, a couple of the local losers caught sight of one of their young women. She was just a teenager at the time. The two goons were about 20 or so." He took a breath, looking at the table.

"Oh, here we go. They grabbed her and assaulted her," said Montrose, anticipating yet another horror story.

"They wanted to, were attempting to put her in their car, but a couple senior tribe members managed to chase them off. The group was in the bog, harvesting cattail roots to eat. Back before they filled in and destroyed the marshes. Anyway, the dipshits smacked around the two older folks, a man and a woman, both about 60 years old. The idiots got some scratches in return from the harvest rakes the tribal members brandished; later the two punks most likely made a return trip in the dark for some payback," Kane said.

"Most likely? You're losing us, Albert," Bodkin said.

"Well, no one outside the tribe knew for sure, as both of the losers were never seen again. The one kid's Dodge Dart was found on the dirt road near the first altercation. One of the punks' dads told the cops his revolver was stolen, most likely by the thieving son. Who knows? If he had it, that disappeared along with him."

"You said outside the tribe...how about within it?" Montrose asked.

"Oh, they knew. Defensive action had been taken. You see, the two morons only saw the gatherers. The peaceful ones, out in the daylight, gathering plant bounty. Not the tribe's protectors; not the warriors who lured the young men to where they wanted, then killed them," Kane said. A moment of quiet followed.

"You seem to know a lot about this, Albert. You must be privy to some special info," Bodkin said finally.

"I was told the details...by one of the warriors who ate them," Kane said.

A longer moment of quiet followed, to the extent that all of them could hear the house shift as the chilled winds outside nudged it.

Kane continued: "The first time we spoke, I told you of Hone, not mentioning the tribal class from which Hone got his name. Hone is, as you guessed, just the name I use for him. The tribal caste of protectors were known as the Honani."

"Honani. Thus the short name Hone. What's his real name?" Bodkin said.

"One of the Kasa's traditional names, but I can't pronounce it. Very long name. Anyway, I said to you Hone was a hunter, a warrior, a protector. All true, but there's more. He was just one of many, one of the Honani."

"Go on."

"In Kasa, the word *Honani* literally means *badger*. Thus the ferocity, the attacks from ambush and from below. And thus the tunnels provided for the rest of the tribe. The navigation underground, and the building of the passages in the first place. A way of life provided for the passive gatherers, the makers of clothing, the cooks. And those specialties were things the Honani didn't excel in. They were provided to the Honani in turn by the non-warriors."

"Badger men? Like part beast?" Montrose said, a little doubt creeping into her voice.

"They were human, part of the tribe, but from a special bloodline. Shorter, wider, stronger. And rare. Don't trivialize it; ever see a wildlife documentary on TV, where a badger defends its lair? Trust me, the Honani didn't do it much differently." Kane paused and looked at both of them, then down again.

"They'd readily kill if they had to. And they believed in consuming the enemy's flesh, in order to collect that energy, to grow stronger."

"Convenient after working up an appetite, I'd bet," Bodkin said.

Kane ignored his comment, and continued. "Over a thousand years ago the Kasa moved to this region of the continent; originally they're from the northern Montana and North Dakota areas, and up a ways into Saskatchewan. Back in that region, over the centuries, the Kasa suffered attacks from some other tribes. Notably the Blackfoot. Heard of them?"

"Sure. Pretty well-known among Native American tribes," Montrose said.

"Raiders," Bodkin said.

"Exactly," Kane said. "Well, from afar the Blackfoot probably figured the tribe to be easy prey. Sheep, basically. But they didn't know what watched over the flock. Didn't know about the Honani."

"Blackfoot for breakfast," Bodkin said.

"Without question. Taught the other raiders to keep their distance. But back to those two punks, and their attempted abduction of the Kasa girl...their return with one or more guns. That's the only time I know about cannibalism occurring in modern day."

"So only when really, really hungry?" Bodkin said.

"Only when in danger, and only after taking out an enemy," Kane said.

"Our currently active Honani, your friend the night stalker, in on that feast?"

"Yes. Hone himself was just a youngster then; as the story goes, that was his first sampling of human."

"But not likely his last," Bodkin said. "So these folks speak – or spoke – English apparently."

"Only enough to just get by with me. I was their only English-speaking contact, after my folks died."

"This Hone speak any English?" Bodkin said.

"Same as his forebears...a smattering of words; his voice is more designed to speak Kasa, so the English words are rough. More like grunts and purrs."

"You speak any Kasa?"

"Just some expressions and terms, not enough to carry on fluent conversation." Kane paused, then looked at the wide rug by the sink. He said, "That's the tunnel exit spot right there, as you guessed. Would you like to peer down into it?"

"I don't think so," Montrose said. "We've had enough surprises on other projects, jobs much more standard than this one. We have a plan we'll stick to, thanks."

"Of course, I doubt he's down below us now," Kane said. "The tunnel system leading from here is not set up for living; just for passing through."

That caused Bodkin to issue half a grin. "Just a way to get to tea and refreshments after a carnivorous feast, huh?"

Kane lifted his palms up, fatigued, with little to say. "I never knew it would go this far."

"Anything else you can tell us that may be of help?"

Kane shook his head. "What are you planning?"

"Since he's a loved one of yours, we can't divulge that, Mr. Kane. For obvious reasons," Montrose said. "Have to play it close to the vest."

"*Loved one.* Hmm. More like a longtime neighbor, or a distant family member; I don't love him, but I do pity him," Kane said. "And I have some big decisions to make regarding this situation."

"Like what?" Bodkin said.

"I have to play it close to the vest myself. Sorry."

"Trying to capsize us would not be advisable, Albert," Bodkin said.

"No worries, Mr. Bodkin. The decisions don't involve you," said Kane, attempting a weak smile. As he and Montrose stood to leave, Bodkin thought he saw a mist come over Kane's eyes. As if the old man had just read the ending of a very sad story.

Ten

They'd parked on the shoulder of the interstate's frontage road, in order to approach the tunnel's hidden opening from the same way they had just before visiting Kane: there'd then be no need to cross the frigid, muddy creek.

Earlier, the three of them had found the tunnel entrance easily. Bodkin simply brought Montrose and Sheba to the spot opposite the creek where the Bryce abduction trail had joined with the creek. From there, they searched the opposite side of the creek. Right at the muddy water's edge. Bodkin figured the creep had a doorway right next to the water; no way to track his scent then, if he could leave the creek and step almost straight into a cave entrance from the water.

But if you knew the exact section to examine, and you had a scenting dog like Sheba, well...minutes into the track they came to the little thatched door. Nothing locking it down other than a wispy tentacle of vine, meant to stop the root, weed, and mud door from lifting up during strong wind gusts. No security at all against the assault they had planned. It would be like a trio of wolfhounds coming after a badger, and following it into its lair. And two of these wolfhounds had guns.

Bodkin had cranked his truck's heater to the maximum, coating their hands with warmth and coaxing healthy blood flow. A dark, cold northern environment awaited them just outside the shelter of the vehicle. Better to increase the initial odds in your favor just a little, before the deep freeze set in. Keep that skin warm; stay flexible, alert, and ready. Needed to be sharp as a tack when going in after an ambitious cannibal.

The truck heater was the first order of business, the espresso the second. Years back, when Montrose first teamed up with Bodkin, she'd found his preoccupation with the brownish black elixir somewhat amusing. Then over time, she stopped putting cream in her coffee, drinking it black like Bodkin did. Next, graduating to straight espresso, down the hatch and chased with plain water. Considering their primary profession – partly bounty hunters, partly seek-and-destroy specialists – the ignition of anxious alertness from the hyper-caffeinated espresso sludge was perfect.

And it was especially perfect under these conditions, maybe more so than at any other time, with the biting frost awaiting them...as well as a nearly 100% likelihood they were about to meet the killer.

Bodkin handed Montrose the first serving of espresso, a steaming capful from a slender, stainless steel thermos. Two near-scalding slugs and the drink was gone. Bodkin had a big chug, then another, then back to Montrose. Once Bodkin had six espresso shots in him and Montrose four, the attitude adjustment was well under way.

"A little left. One more?" Bodkin asked.

"No, the gulps I've had should do the trick. Save the rest for our victory dance afterward," Montrose said.

From an insulated backpack Montrose removed two smaller cases, and after unzipping one, handed Bodkin the device from inside it. Night vision goggles, U.S. Marine Corps issue, the same design used by Force Recon commandos. The eyewear would illuminate the nighttime world for them just enough to get the job done. They'd been through the process before; outside in the dark the surroundings would brighten up to look simply like an overcast day, and improve to a less bright, dim grey inside of a dark cave. Not perfect visibility, but enough to help fulfill the mission: fix on the target and squeeze the trigger.

They each slipped on lightweight wool balaclavas, head coverings that left only their faces showing; the straps of the night vision goggles were then fit snugly on top of the wool fabric. Next they donned tight leather shooting gloves, the thin insulation enough to stave off cold for a brief period only. They both hoped to have this operation wrapped up before the cold had time to torture them in earnest. Let the cold take over, and among other things, their trigger fingers would no longer work. Not good.

Bodkin reached into the backseat of the extended-cab truck, caressing Sheba's head and neck for a moment. Then he clicked the latch on her collar, removed it from her and flipped it to the floor. In so doing there'd be no collar for an assailant to latch onto in a full-contact fight, if it came down to that. The gesture was significant to the wolf-dog, after years of experience in similar situations: it signaled time for action. Shimmers of excitement traveled through her muscles. Bodkin withdrew from a pocket the bone shard, the lost portion of Hone's weapon. He held it close to Sheba's face, and she bumped her nose against it, breathing in and marking the scent. The shimmers in Sheba's body increased, and the brightness in the animal's eyes increased ever so slightly.

In the close quarters they'd soon navigate, a rifle or a full-size shotgun would be unmanageable, and could truly be a liability as they maneuvered it around sharp bends and cramped spaces. As an alternative, Montrose would carry her pistol, a .40-caliber semiautomatic, 15 shots in the inserted magazine. An additional three magazines, stuffed to the top with shiny, hollow-point cartridges, were secured in compartments on her holster's belt, next to her sheath knife. Bodkin carried his top choice, a 12-gauge shotgun, albeit with a pistol grip in place of a standard, full-size butt stock. The barrel was a short 18 inches, and its cavernous muzzle provided a wide passageway from which handfuls of buckshot could fly. He had nine cartridges resting in the gun's tube, awaiting explosive activation. Another five shells were stored on his own belt; considering the shells in the gun already, each capable of a blast powerful enough to knock down an elk, he was pretty sure he'd never need the extras.

In addition, like Gladdis, he wore steel-toed hiking boots. If he ran out of ammo, and she couldn't put the hit on the attacker with the handgun, he could always just kick at the enemy instead. He felt a flicker of amusement at the thought, but he shouldn't have. It was actually intuition speaking.

They stepped from the truck and looked around the dark setting, goggles still shifted up on their foreheads. Lights glowed from massive houses, row after row, straight ahead of them a few hundred yards; non-stop freeway clamor thundered behind them. Noise from the highway might actually be a good thing in this case: it would help mask whatever slight sounds they made on their way to the tunnel entrance. The breeze picked up for a moment, sending a subzero stroke of wind against their faces.

"Can we delay tonight's plan, and just come back in the warm spring weather for this? When all the snow's melted?" Montrose said. "Be more enjoyable."

"I thought you were a certified outdoor survival expert," Bodkin said.

"But I prefer 80 and sunny."

"But then we'll be battling the creep and a million

mosquitoes at the same time," Bodkin said. "Plus, if we do it now, there'll be less chance of people getting eaten in the near future."

"There's that cannibalism thing again," Montrose said. "All right. Who knows, maybe we'll warm up."

"Hope so. Less icy wind down in deep, dark, spooky tunnel systems," Bodkin said. "Should help."

Maneuvering their feet deftly through the powder, avoiding any crunchy branches or dry leaves, they began their approach.

Eleven

The tunnel system's air flowed at a gentle, almost peaceful pace. This was no dark dungeon. The delicate airstream was pushing out old air and replacing it with new. The bitter cold had largely disappeared this far underground, but every few seconds Bodkin felt a brush of icy air, probably from above ground. Fresh. The ventilation of this tunnel was either a nicely convenient find for the Kasa tribe, or a very ingenious design they'd set up.

Tiny candles, maybe six or seven of them, illuminated the nearby section of cavern. The base of each looked like a thick ball of dried mud, with a twisted wick of weeds and roots of some kind extending out, tipped with a small flame. Each flame wiggled toward the air movement's direction, as if pointing the way. Bodkin could smell the burning of animal fats – similar to when he cooked wild game in a frying pan – floating around the tunnel. Probably what the wicks were coated with to burn low and slow. No time to think about it though.

They moved forward, shotgun and pistol held relaxed but ready, the illumination gathered from the night vision goggles showing brightly near the candles, but as just a faint grey up ahead. Better than complete darkness, but not much.

The descent into the tunnel system had been easy. Hone – or perhaps tribe members long before his time – had set up the ladder system leading their way down to be as usable as possible. Where roots didn't naturally occur, they had interwoven small vine ropes with the larger of the roots; simple to clutch, almost indestructible in strength.

Bodkin went down first – he'd insisted upon it. They didn't know if the hungry killer waited below with a spear, knife, or more likely, the chopper club thing he was so attached to. As Bodkin descended, Montrose waited above. Cool in demeanor but not calm, hand cannon on fire and pointed at the ground. Ready to point down into the entrance and rain holy hell on Bodkin's attacker, 15 shots as fast as she could pull the trigger, if such an event went down. It didn't.

Bodkin had lifted the covering to the tunnel entrance as soundlessly as possible, his ability to stay silent a well-developed skill. Years of hunting deer at point-blank ranges with bow and arrow had helped, and over time the urge to not be slain by bad guys had enhanced the process. Maintaining silence upon entry into the primitive hideout, just like the climb down that followed it, also turned out to be easy. The owner of the mud-weed-vine lid had made it so. On the hatch's simple hinges, the creep had applied some kind of grease or oil as a lubricant – another prehistoric method of achieving stealth; no sound occurred as Bodkin had lifted the door.

Once the tunnel's door was fully open, Sheba had to be restrained. She'd inhaled the smell of the bone blade, containing traces of Hone on them. The understanding being that odor signified the enemy, and the scent wafted to her here in thick waves. She'd inched toward the tunnel's entrance, ready to plunge in and seize the prey, a rumbling vibrating inside her. Bodkin gripped fur along her neck, yanked it, and put his face close to hers.

"Full attack, girl," he'd said to her. The wolf dog's eyes had caught a glow from the moonlight, and a tiny flicker of extra energy surged in them as he said it. The command only meant one thing. Bodkin had clutched her skin tighter, looking into the lupine eyes, then had relaxed the grip and stroked her head. She'd twitched with extra energy, now wound tight; the twitchy state pleased Bodkin. He then said nothing more to his dog, turning away and proceeding with the entry into the lair.

The coast was clear so far, and Montrose joined Bodkin as he watched for motion, her pistol holstered and her gymnast abilities helping her to reach Bodkin's side in seconds. Pistol back out. They moved forward in the tunnel, which was almost six feet high and perhaps eight feet wide. They progressed to the edge of what looked like an enlarging of the tunnel, maybe a 16-foot wide expanse, approximately 20 feet long, the ceiling there reaching a full 12 feet. Three wall-mounted candles burned there, the flames of each doing a lazy dance. Hone's main living quarters would be an obvious guess.

There'd been no way to know if Hone would be in the lair at all; he could have been out hunting. And killing. Seemed as though he'd done a lot of that lately.

But, no. It turned out there'd be no delay or postponement of the showdown. Hone almost certainly was here.

It appeared they'd walked in on him while he was cooking something up. Thirty feet or so from where they'd dropped down to the tunnel's floor, a small pile of red coals pulsed beneath a big clay pot. The pot was held up in four spots by small boulders, leaving enough room to feed twigs and branches into the fire. A handful of brush was to the side of the cooking setup; some birch, oak, and elm branches it looked like, ready to refuel the cooking process.

A stew of some kind, Bodkin concluded. He glanced at the contents, then back up to the widening in the tunnel. There was no sense in letting distractions interfere, so Bodkin never looked back down. But in that second he saw seeds and leaves floating at the top of the broth, the leaves probably from dandelions. A large bone, already thoroughly cooked, had rested in the stew as well. Bodkin was pretty sure he knew what type of bone.

This Hone bastard has to go.

Inching along, progressing bit by bit, Bodkin set each step down with a gingerly touch, placing footfalls squarely in the center area of the boot. Minimizing noise, a skill perfected long ago. Behind him, Montrose made motions equally absent of sound. The two stopped every few moments, holding still. Listening, with miniscule crackles from the smoldering coals the only sound.

Listening, and watching. Inspecting the primitive cavern. The night vision goggles illuminated the dark spots to the level of a typical person's vision during a severely overcast day; the areas with candles were visible as if a 60-watt bulb were burning there. But without the goggles, the two would be able to see only dim shapes in the candlelight, and nothing at all in the unlit sections. Best not to lose the goggles.

A miniature alcove had been dug into the tunnel wall, with a pair of shelves sculpted into it. Small tools of both stone and bone rested on the shelves, along with a smattering of food sources. Handfuls of acorns were piled on one, and a little bowl of ground-up meal sat on another. A momentary look at it suggested pulverized pine cones. Some other mixed seeds, probably from wildflowers, were stacked behind the bowl.

Bodkin noticed a string of ornaments wrapped on a wooden hook in the alcove. Tribal jewelry of some kind, he thought at first, then he focused on them once again.

Ornate in various colors and round in shape, the ornaments didn't appear to be ancient at all. Appeared to be new, somehow. He looked closer, the goggles not helping for such a detailed examination. Then it became clear to Bodkin: the shapes were plastic.

Plastic beads. The kind certain circles wore as decoration in modern times. New age enthusiasts, musicians, artists. Here the beads were being kept as souvenirs, maybe to remember, to relive, one of Hone's kills.

She was known as the Bright-eyed Beadster.

The words spoken by Francine Babbitt's sister, Tina, came back to him. *When the county built the paved paths through the wetland, she took to them. Trying to embrace nature as she wandered, I guess.*

Right into the path of the supposed tribal legend. Hone, the mystical warrior, whose predecessors were said to fight off marauding Blackfoot braves. Out here in the wetland, preying on a recovering drug addict, a woman barely out of her teens. She stood just over five feet tall. Most likely had never been in a fight in her life. *A gentle soul*, her sister had said. And this virtuous protector of the tribe, of all things good, had decided to kill and abduct her. Probably butchered and consumed her. Just as he had likely done to the wife of a now-grieving husband nearby; as he had done to a little kid's mom.

We'll see how much of a mighty warrior you are, Cave Man.

Bodkin exchanged a glance with Montrose – she'd taken in the sight of the beads too – and they continued to inch forward. Into the open area in the tunnel, the system's town square.

They inspected the open space. More decorations, most of them looking more like authentic artwork a primitive tribe might design. Weeds twisted together to make masks, some almost amusing. Dried out wildflowers, arranged in ornate sculptures. Like the ones around Kane's souvenir spear. A few tiny, varnished skulls, mostly rodents. One Bodkin identified as a coyote skull, another a fox skull. Some from gophers and groundhogs. *Very charming, Hone, you get an A+ for interior decorating.*

Montrose looked from the compelling skull and mask collection, and let her eyes wander along the wall. Another couple of shelves, with a few mugs and bowls long ago squished into shape from clay, then probably hardened by placing them right in a bed of hot coals.

Higher up, a leather tarp hung from the wall, sections stitched together from what looked like pieces of deer hide. A couple of duffle bag-style containers hung beneath the tarp; also looked to be deer hide. Maybe the furs from a few coyotes connected together, hard to tell. Up the wall beyond that point it was pitch dark, and the illumination from the goggles allowed her to make out some kind of webbing material. Maybe more tools, or skulls, stowed up there for future use. The Kasa's version of an attic. Who could tell?

Montrose started to turn away, to touch base via eye contact with Bodkin; if he estimated it was all clear here, they'd have to push on ahead, where the tunnel once again grew narrow. Fun. Started to turn away, when some of the chill only adrenaline can deliver began to spread through her.

In a split-second, Montrose processed it. The tarp hanging from the wall had a consistent, rawhide finish until it reached the upper left corner. In that corner, the hide finish changed from consistent, tanned leather, to a more furry finish. Seemed like...

A shoulder. With a furry arm attached. She faced it again, just as both duffle-type leather bags beneath the tarp started to move. To fold in the middle. To bend like a pair of knees; one of the leather bags started to rotate toward them. A massive leg, flexing at the knee. Ready to spring.

As the tarp with the shoulder and arm burst into

movement, the webbing material up above it grew wider, and surged downward. Like the talon of a raptor clutching its victim, the net twirled down onto Montrose.

"Lee!" she screamed. At the same time Montrose squeezed off a shot as the net engulfed her hand, the flash exploding the tunnel into full light for an instant and the bullet thudding with no consequence into the mud wall. Teeth of some kind within the net – thorns – bit into her skin.

Bodkin had the 12-gauge up before the report from her pistol ended, directing the bead at the bulk of skin and leather which had just dropped next to her from above. The form had a club held overhead, a bright blade sticking out either side of the weapon's head. The club came down as Montrose rolled and Bodkin blasted his gun.

Hone was struck in the hip by just two of the buckshot load's many wicked pellets, saved partly by his forward motion as he sliced at the rolling Montrose. Bodkin jacked another cartridge into the boom stick as Hone sprung the 13 feet between them with one step and a big leap. Hone flew with the leg strength of a kangaroo above Bodkin, descending for the kill.

The club came down, and Bodkin had to honor the chop instead of shoot. He blocked the club arcing down from above, the bone clacking on the metal gun material. Hone smashed into Bodkin with the downward momentum, Bodkin whirling to deflect the force. Hone was in the process of being thrown off, but he clutched Bodkin's gun and tore it from his hands. He pitched it off into the darkness, turning back to Bodkin and getting a two-handed grip on his weapon with its bone blade. The instant he did it, instead of the victim running as Hone was accustomed to, this one moved up. Hone felt a lightning bolt of pain shock his knee; he never saw the motion of the kick. He tried to reset himself on his good leg, to make the killing whack, when stars ignited in his eyes.

Bodkin's steel-toed boot had clipped the Hone freak under the chin, though not as fully as Bodkin wanted. But Hone dropped his club, and as he bent to grab it, Bodkin kicked him again, this time in the forehead. The cave dweller grunted, then sprung again. Hone clamped onto Bodkin and tried to bite his face; Bodkin could see sharpened teeth closing toward the goggles. As Bodkin clasped Hone's leather top and pitched him, Hone tore off Bodkin's night vision goggles. Hone hit the nearest wall, and Bodkin searched the floor, now mostly dark, for his goggles and shotgun. No dice, and no time.

He looked ahead; the image of Hone was rising back up, now just a shadowy figure in the sparse candlelight. Bodkin couldn't see the sharpened teeth on the monster, but now knew they were there. Sharp, like the teeth of a badger. Nice touch.

"OK, Gladdis?" Bodkin barked.

"So far yes, just a second and I'll waste him," Montrose growled; Bodkin could hear the net thing on her getting sliced apart with her combat knife. His own skinning knife was at his house. Great. They were going after an unarmed wild man, and they both had guns. How hard could it be? Bodkin had halfway figured the geek would run away, escape from the tunnel somehow.

The geek, the very burly geek, now positioned himself in front of Bodkin. Hone's club was on the ground behind Bodkin, and he likely wanted that thing back. Bodkin figured if he let Hone get the bladed club, both he and Gladdis were basically Hone's next prime rib dinner. With those sharpened teeth savoring the feast.

"Shoot yet?" Bodkin said to Montrose, his voice

elevated with the urgency and echoing in the close quarters.

"Almost," Montrose said, matching his voice's urgency, the slicing with her knife continuing, a gasp of pain as thorns in the net material sliced across her hands.

"Can I grab the gun from you quick?" Bodkin said, still fixing on the silhouette of Hone, waiting for another charge.

"Nope, it's still tangled up," Montrose snarled.

"Cool, keep cutting, I got him," Bodkin said. So we do it the hard way, he thought to himself. Hand-to-hand. Evaluating the shape of Hone. Oh yeah, just like that, we've got him. Good God.

More a hunched over gorilla than a man, the outline of Hone definitely leaned toward the Neanderthal. *You'll know him when you see him.*

Bodkin had battled with so many men before. Between street fighting, wrestling, more street fighting, and finally bounty hunting, he'd went up against all shapes and sizes, hand-to-hand. Not quite shaped like this before, though. Well, a couple of Hell's Outcasts had been, and he'd thumped them. So...

In two more seconds, his positive attitude secured itself. Motivation reinforcement: win this thing, and you collect a paycheck. His assurance inched up. Beat this creep, you wrap up this assignment...you get out of the cold that much sooner. The assurance crept up some more. Lose this struggle, and you get butchered and eaten by this thing in front of you.

Bodkin's motivation came back in full force.

Just in time, too. Hone lowered his head, exhaled a huff, a sound between a cough and a roar, and charged.

Wild man versus the modern, tough guy, ex-wrestler jock. Betting men would go with the wild man every time. And not knowing the fighting arts, those bettors would lose the bet more often than not.

Hone, the wild man, was a master of stealth and ambush. Pragmatic learning had taught him how to hunt down prey, both animal and human, with deceit and the cover of weather and brush. Hands-on savagery. But he was more of a weapon-wielder; no training whatsoever in unarmed combat. No tricks, no tactics, just ferocity. The kind that gets spent in seconds when fighting. His last chance was size, but the two men weighed about the same. Hone had no advantage there.

Other than sharpened teeth, Bodkin possessed every dangerous trait and skill Hone did. But in addition to those, so much more that could be put to use in a struggle. In earlier years, he'd learned moves from some of the best wrestling coaches in the country. And he'd then used those moves as he wrestled some of the toughest guys in the entire world. In contrast, Hone's victims were, without fail, relative weaklings in comparison. Plus, he customarily snuck up and put a bone blade through their brain, so he got no grappling experience from that.

Hone was strong, very capable of carrying carcasses he'd harvested. Bodkin could carry deer the same size if he had to, and he had. But additionally, Bodkin performed workouts every week with massive, hulking dumbbells and barbells. He could deadlift the equivalent of he and Hone put together from the floor, the huge iron disks jiggling against gravity's pull as he pulled it up and held it. And held it some more. Just for recreation and fitness.

There was no way Hone, hunkering in his tunnel, stewing with hatred of the outside world, could ever approximate it.

Bodkin currently practiced judo and jiu-jitsu for the throws and joint locks. Taught himself taekwondo kicks;

Hone had just felt three of them, from steel-toed boots
no less. His current-day martial arts practice was not
done to compete in tournaments; it was to get better at
injuring people. People like the Hell's Outcasts he'd just
thought about. And murderers like Hone.

It was a match between the hungry, frantic wild man
versus the perfectly fortified, highly trained modern
fighter. The contest didn't last long. Hone, almost
laughingly, tried to tackle Bodkin at first. Bodkin, a
former college wrestler, thus an expert at leg tackle
defense. Bodkin parried and kneed Hone in the face,
waited until he came up, then stepped in close and
tagged his brow bone with a roundhouse elbow.

Hone backed off, tried to claw at Bodkin's face, and
was sent twirling to the tunnel's floor, clutching his
twisted wrist. The wild man got back up. A lunge, a left
jab into his nose. Hone stepped back, now streaming
blood from both his nose and hip.

"I'm free, Lee!" Montrose then said. He was about to
coordinate dropping to the floor as she put five or six
shots through Hone's center of mass. Instead, Hone
leapt at Bodkin. In the worst way he could. He leapt
high, and as Bodkin ducked, Hone landed across his
shoulders.

In an unarmed struggle, Bodkin could punch, elbow,
twist, knee, stomp, and kick. But nothing suited him
better than launching the opponent up high into the air,
using the most classic of wrestling takedowns, the
double-leg tackle. Then pile-driving the hapless
opponent to whatever surface lay at their feet. With all of
the opponent's weight, and his, crashing down.

Everybody's got a plan, until they get body slammed.

Bodkin's policy, and it had rarely failed him in a
fight. He then obliged the ferocious Hone, slamming
him.

On the way to the tunnel's floor, Bodkin leapt his own feet completely up and out from the ground, to contribute to the fullest extent possible his bodyweight. At the same time, he angled Hone's head and shoulders down, and Hone's lower body up. Result: the impact almost completely absorbed by Hone's head.

After the thumping landing and the resulting bounce, Bodkin jumped up. Hone was stunned, and started to roll over. Bodkin seized his deerskin collar from behind, then hauled back and swept Hone's body up and completely off the floor.

Powerlifting style.

Bodkin used the secured position, back and away from his opponent's clawing nails, by twirling Hone in the air and into the wall, a resounding thud barely done when Bodkin did the same back to the floor. Hone's breath was audibly expelled from his body, unable to suck in any more before he was crashed back into the wall. Then pitched straight ahead, as far from Montrose and himself as Bodkin could manage. Bodkin heard Hone land, flesh hitting packed earth. Bodkin then resumed his scramble for his night vision goggles. And his 12-gauge.

"To your left Lee," Montrose urged. Bodkin touched the goggles then, scooped them up and thrust them onto his head. Then back down, to the shotgun. And up, with the fresh shell fed into the chamber moments ago.

A split-second glance at Montrose found her free of the net, pistol up and pointing. He glanced back to where he had thrown Hone.

Out of the main living area and around the bend in the tunnel, out of sight from where Montrose stood, the cannibal was just starting to rise from the floor. He was clearly disoriented, the predator posture now gone, the alertness diminished. Through the near-darkness, he looked in Bodkin's direction, his chest heaving with exhaustion, his face seeming to reflect defeat.

"Got a favorite prayer?" said Bodkin, taking a step forward, the bead on the shotgun barrel trained on the killer's chest. As he did it he heard Montrose scramble up behind him. Her breath, like Bodkin's, labored from the exertion, but it was an old routine for them. Ignore the pain and commandeer the situation.

For the first time, Hone spoke. It sounded to Bodkin like what he imagined the voice of a dog might come out as, if it was trained to speak human words. A dog or, for that matter, a badger.

"Ay sahrve...day sahrve me," the voice growled.

Bodkin had the gun trained on the other man, and had applied the tiniest pressure on the trigger. Ready to blast. He reduced it, just a little. What was the cannibal trying to say? Hone, stooped over, looking beaten and hopeless, spoke again, and Bodkin then caught it.

"Sahrve me."

Starve me. They starve me.

The descriptions they'd heard, from both Kane and Lanky, came back to Bodkin: the maple and honey locust trees, along with the black walnut trees, the berries, the endless supply of subsistence fish...all removed, the bounty they provided dried up. Abundance for generations, for thousands of years, then suddenly nothing. Bodkin kept his finger on the trigger, but relaxed it.

"What are you waiting for, Lee?" Montrose said.

Bodkin kept the muzzle pointed at Hone, and didn't reply for a few seconds. At times Bodkin had wished he were born a sadist, a sociopath. It would have been so much easier.

"Letting him catch his breath, so we can have another go-round?" asked Montrose, the disbelief in her voice coming through.

"How do you apprehend something like this?" Bodkin said finally. He couldn't believe he was hesitating; the instant he had the chance, the predator in front of them would kill them both.

"Apprehend? You don't. He gets ahold of that axe thing he'll try again to bury it in our brains. Then probably eat us."

"Since when have we become executioners?" Bodkin said. "He's unarmed and helpless."

Bodkin peered directly at Hone, and raised his voice a little. "This is your chance to surrender. Do you understand what I mean by the word 'surrender'?" Bodkin said.

"Bodkin, have you lost your mind?" Montrose hissed.

"He's done for. He's got nothing left," Bodkin replied. "Should we get him down and hog-tie him?"

"Step aside and let me finish this standoff," Montrose said, adjusting the .40-caliber in her grip. He knew Gladdis. She'd shoot the guy as many times as it took to put him down, and he had to admit, that was logical given the situation. Bodkin started to doubt his will to kill the man in front of him, the urge which had burned so bright just seconds ago. Now, it seemed like murder. Had to decide, quickly...but as it turned out, he didn't have long to think.

Bodkin glanced at Montrose, about to explain his thoughts; Hone took the opportunity and sprung into action. Gladdis had been right, Bodkin thought in that instant; Hone had simply been catching his breath, getting back his bearings.

The predator lunged for the wall, to a grinding stone resting on a shelf there. He grabbed it, and with a flourish of deadly motion, Hone sent the grapefruit-sized rock with sizzling speed at Bodkin. Bodkin dropped to the right, heading for the ground, before the stone slammed into the top of his shoulder girdle, thunking off the muscle and bone and twisting him back. The surprise and impact of the thrown missile steered a blast from his shotgun into the clay of the tunnel's ceiling.

His burst was inaccurate, but the three bullets Montrose shot were not. Before Bodkin's shotgun thunder had even left the caverns of their ears, Montrose planted slugs in Hone's belly, arm, and chest, each blast lighting up the tunnel, the explosive sounds nearly as loud as the 12-gauge.

But Hone didn't drop. He instead crouched and leapt upward, reaching, aiming at an escape portal above. Hone grasped handles fashioned from vines on either side of the portal, blood drops from his hip, nose, and three new bullet wounds splashing back to the dirt below; he smacked a grass and twig exit door away with the top of his head, and scrambled out into the cold, snowy darkness above ground.

Bodkin was already back on his feet, ignoring the bleeding dent in his skin at the clavicle; he pumped a fresh load of buckshot into the gun's chamber while looking at Montrose, her own weapon still in position and eager to again find its target.

"You OK?" Bodkin said, the sound of his voice barely audible to their ringing ears after the gunfire. Montrose just nodded, then glanced away from Bodkin. Up to the open escape hole of Hone's lair, down which the icy winter breeze now floated to embrace them.

Twelve

"Follow him through that hole, or go back and chase him from the main entrance?" Montrose said.

Bodkin looked in the direction of the portal, but didn't make a move. "I don't think we'll need to do either, Blondie," he said.

Montrose looked at Bodkin askance for a couple of seconds. "He's unarmed; let's finish this thing now," Montrose said. Then she paused, "Or should we let him weaken? The weather will get him. With only that sleeveless top on, he'll freeze."

"I don't think he'll get the chance to."

Montrose was about to ask for clarification, but the sounds from above reached them. She knew immediately what Bodkin had assumed.

Hone was bleeding, weakening, exhausted. And he now had no weapon; the stone he'd thrown rested on the mud floor behind them. His beloved blade-wielding club lay abandoned here in the tunnel. And he'd scrambled out of his lair, the predator now wounded, careless, and unarmed. To where another predator waited for him.

He was dead meat.

Drifting down to them had been the half-roar that Hone had issued before. The challenge, the war cry, responding to an attack.

Huh. Good luck, Hone buddy. He'd need more than bluster for what awaited him.

Then a gurgle echoed down into the tunnel, during what sounded like a short struggle. Overpowered, voicing the terror of it, not the pain. What Bodkin pictured happening to Hone would involve very little pain.

Full attack, girl. The command only meant one thing. The killer, now the prey, had been flushed out like a rabbit by beagles. To another hunter lying in wait.

Any dog could have heard the struggles below, sensing its master was in danger. But Sheba was far more alert than a standard dog, her protective urges extreme, her switch to ultra-violence a hair trigger. If Bodkin hadn't given Sheba the command, she probably would have killed Hone anyway.

"For what it was worth, I gave him a chance to surrender," Bodkin said.

"Guess he really didn't want to be hog-tied," Montrose said. She paused for a moment, catching her breath. Bodkin did the same. "You think that's it?" she said.

"You know as well as I do what those sounds meant," Bodkin replied. She nodded.

Montrose holstered her pistol, and Bodkin put his boom stick on safety. There'd be no more shooting tonight.

"I forgot to ask: are *you* OK?" Montrose said.

"Ah, not sure yet. That stone thumped me good. Collarbone might be broken," Bodkin said.

"Didn't you break one years back? In a wrestling match?"

"Um, I think that was in a street fight. It was the other one though."

"Should even you out."

They waited another minute, listening. Then Bodkin and Montrose maneuvered back through the tunnel, from whence they came to the main entrance, to exit and observe the horror up top.

***

"The old saber-toothed safety net," Montrose said. "Hone was flushed out, just like you figured."

"Yep, although getting him to that point was harder than planned," Bodkin said, moving his arm in a slow, careful circle. Agony setting in, a few places on his body affected...but at least they had lived.

The two of them looked over at the canine. Sheba was not your standard dog. Due to her training, and to something which naturally rumbled around inside her heart, the unarmed combatant was at a distinct disadvantage. She sometimes went for a mortal enemy's arms, hands, face, or throat. Regardless, all initial attacks were meant to make the victim twist, turn, or cower, in order to get to her objective: the base of the skull, where it meets the neck in back – where the brain stem is located. Long, sharp teeth plunge in, a shake or two or three, and the victim is done. No chance of the bad guy making one last stab with his knife or blasting a final shot with a handgun. The brainstem bite, inspired by the standard killing method of the grizzly bear, was an attack only for the most serious of conditions, with the most dangerous of adversaries...typical of those Bodkin and Montrose pursued.

Sheba was companion, tracker, and protector. But she was also a purposeful killer. Definitely not your standard dog.

"Looks like one of your bullets connected with his midsection, the other up high on the chest. He was probably dead on his feet anyway," Bodkin said, looking at the blood streams melting away snow around Hone's body. He watched Sheba, as she pranced back and forth, still eyeing Hone.

"No sense taking a chance," Montrose said.

He looked from the dog over to Hone, the bulky frame now limp, just a short while ago filled with the violence of a demon and the cunning of a commando.

"I agree, definitely no sense in that," Bodkin said.

***

"What happened?" Police Captain Norman Jenkins asked.

"Some beating, some shooting, some biting," Bodkin said into his phone.

"Biting?"

"You stated this was catch-as-catch-can, Captain Jenkins. Whatever it takes. That's what we did. Anyway, we'll be waiting by the frontage road and Mineral Street," Bodkin said, before signing off and putting his phone away.

***

The three of them started off in the direction of the truck; had to drive over to the meeting spot with the police. After a few steps, Bodkin felt Montrose stop. He followed suit. A lone figure stood still 50 yards ahead and to the west. Toward the bulk of the wetland. Silhouetted against the snow, the shape of the man was easy to make out. As was the slender barrel of the rifle slung across his back.

Bodkin heard Montrose move her jacket off to the side, away from her hip. The snap on her holster popped, the gun ready to be drawn. Again. Bodkin readjusted his grip on the 12-gauge. Its safety could be clicked off in an instant, an assailant cut in half if need be. In this case, he suspected it wouldn't be required.

"Easy girl," he said to Sheba, touching her. She was

still jumpy, just coming off mortal combat as she had. He stepped forward to meet the figure in the dark, Montrose doing the same, just hanging back a bit to present a more complex target if shooting took place.

"I assume that's Hone piled up over there," Albert Kane said, looking past Bodkin.

"It is."

"I had no idea you two were coming here tonight."

Bodkin nodded. Montrose just looked at Kane with a steady gaze.

"It had to be done," Kane said, clutching the rifle strap over his shoulder. He reached a mitten-covered hand up and adjusted the thick wool cap on his head. Montrose stepped up next to her partner, still watching him, watching the rifle on his shoulder.

"You come here to save him?" Montrose said.

"I came here to kill him," Kane replied. "But it looks like that's no longer needed."

"Kill him? I thought he was your friend," Bodkin said.

"He was. But you can't go around taking people. Can't be eating them."

Bodkin and Montrose said nothing, waiting.

"Your first visit tipped me off," Kane said. "In between now and then, he visited me. His own eyes confirmed it, after I asked him. He wouldn't answer me, but he couldn't hide it. I tried to urge him to leave, like any nomad should. To go to a rural area, the wilderness. It would have been so plentiful for him. But he thought this land was his. I knew right then and there I had to end it."

"Albert —," began Bodkin. Kane walked past them, the gait of a senior made even more challenging by the gigantic boots, the heavy winter clothing. They watched as Kane approached the body of Hone, then as the grey shape of Kane outlined against the snow hunched over, hands on knees. His head hung down, a final silent goodbye.

Bodkin looked at Montrose; she met his eyes, looked back over at Kane, then down at the snow. Bodkin did the same. The only point in this whole assignment where he didn't know what to do. He thought of walking over to Kane, but couldn't decide. In a minute, Kane straightened up. He stepped away from the corpse, but didn't come back in the direction of Bodkin and his partner. He walked diagonally, off the nearest path, through the most dense of weeds. More directly to his house, but rough going. Avoiding the two of them.

Bodkin pondered it for a second, but knew he and Montrose hadn't been hired to save the world. They couldn't anyway.

He looked further across the wetland, the weeds, the frozen puddles. Over to the big development. The huge houses. Until tonight, the residents inside each house had been potential prey for Hone, for his persistent hunger. Probably for revenge too; he had been raised in a class of protectors, but there was nobody left to protect.

The residents were now relieved of that threat, but most likely oblivious to it. In house after house, lights burned, both upstairs and downstairs, televisions mesmerizing the inhabitants as another world went on, right outside their doors.

"More houses on that ridge now than there are trees," Montrose said.

Bodkin took one last look at the grandiose section of suburbia, then turned to his partner.

"Times change," he said, feigning indifference with a shrug. The tragedy of all that had happened wasn't lost on either of them. But their work here was done; time to meet up with the cops and get their paycheck approved.

"Shall we?" Bodkin said.

Montrose clipped her holster shut, and reached over and up, wrapping an arm around his neck. He hugged her back; they'd lived through another one, never a guarantee. Then the three of them, man, woman, and dog, began their trudge across the field of powdery snow.

The frigid winter renewed its presence as they walked. A strong arctic gust brushed across the wetland, helping to chill the adrenaline and subdue the sadness.

###

Red Fang

One

For as long as humankind has existed, it has been hunted. On African savannas, in the Australian outback, and amid tropical rainforests south of the equator, numerous predators see the upright human being as a food source. On occasion, people are targeted as prey even in the burly, well-equipped lands of the north.

People of the far north can be a hearty bunch, especially the ones who venture into the wintery outdoors. Between subzero temps, ice-covered surfaces, whistling winds, and blizzard whiteouts, it sometimes seems like northern adventurers can survive anything. And they often do.

Until their time is up.

Chuck Halvorsen felt lucky this Sunday morning, but he was wrong. His time was up. With two game birds in the bag already, he figured he should be able to wrap up a successful hunt within the hour. Just one more bird would be perfect, would make for a perfect wild game feast. Maybe even next weekend with friends. So why not go for one more? The December weather was mild so far, but a cold front was reportedly coming in tomorrow. Predictions said it would top out at only 4 degrees Fahrenheit or so. The lower temps coupled with a steady breeze coming off Lake Superior would make for nippy conditions, both up in the hills where he hunted, as well as down below in town, on the lakeshore. Today, however, was nearly tropical in comparison. It would hit a high of 12°F...balmy for Northern Minnesota in December. Good idea to get in this hunt today, while still pleasant.

Valiant, his Brittany Spaniel, zig-zagged through the thorn bushes in front of him, searching for the sighting or smell of another grouse. The dog had located the other two birds early in their hunt, and with each had went into a disciplined point at the birds' scent. Both shots had been easy for Halvorsen: he had time to set up before each bird burst into flight. His over-and-under shotgun had popped once, and the first bird had crumpled in the air and dropped. The second critter was dispatched in a similar manner. Smooth swing with the shotgun, lead the bird just enough, and squeeze off the sure kill shot. Two shells, two birds: the Chuck Halvorsen way. He'd been hunting grouse most of his 63 years, and the precision shooting had been developed long ago. He still had it.

Valiant maneuvered ahead, and with gun barrels held up high to avoid the brush, Halvorsen followed.

At first he thought the dog was stopping due to spotting a bird; that it had detected prey, and was about to set it up for harvest by its master. In actuality, the opposite predator-prey relationship was now taking place. Valiant froze, then ducked his head to peer under a mass of thorns, viewing nearby motion. The dog then yelped, tucked its tail, and ran back to Halvorsen. Actually, ran *behind* him, cowering there for protection.

Like poisonous leaves tumbling from a contaminated tree, the dark shapes materialized from the thicket, four-legged marauders standing out against the backdrop of pristine white snow. A few came straight at Halvorsen and his pet, others went to the right. Still more veered off to the left. All while a single one of the predators – a special one – stayed back, still out of sight. And waited.

How many creatures had closed in Halvorsen couldn't exactly tell, considering all the adrenaline shooting through his system. The beasts had now surrounded the two of them. Pair after pair of determined amber eyes fixed on him and his animal, and he would have guessed a dozen, at least.

Yes, at least. If he'd had time to count them – being the creatures that they were, they denied him the chance – he would have counted exactly 22. A lifetime in the forests of Northern Minnesota had presented plenty of wolf sightings, but none of the wolves had ever looked quite like the ones facing him down now. Never so big. Or so menacing. A massive, organized pack of them, against one man, a medium-sized dog, and six shotgun shells. Not odds to count on.

In a fast, instinctive switch from hunter to defender, Halvorsen resolved to stand his ground – not that he had much choice. He'd be aggressive and fight back; if any of these things rushed forward to grab him or his dog, he'd blast it with the shotgun. The fact that only two shots total could fit in the gun's chambers wasn't a concern; thoughts that far into the future were now impossible. Deal with the present, take it moment by moment, and focus: the first one to step up would be taken out with a burst of lead, as so many birds had been over the decades – Chuck Halvorsen style.

The wolves held their position, bristling with menace, eyes fixed on the two of them. Subdued growls rumbled from the circle. Thick fur coats shimmered in the winter sun and gentle breeze, all colored in similar fashion with brown, tan, and yellow hair intermixed, light grey along the back, black highlights around the eyes and mouth. They looked somewhat like the local timber wolves...only much larger.

Halvorsen saw another motion from the dense brush; he glanced at it then away, went back to surveying the pack for the one that would rush first, the one who'd get the first face-full of birdshot. He turned his head and looked at the new arrival again, but only after several of the wolves confronting them redirected their fixed stares. Looking over in deference to the dark bulk which now emerged into the clearing. Another wolf.

This one was larger still, and colored differently. A dark charcoal, from snout to tail, no mottling. Its eyes also glimmered a lively amber, but seemed to burn with a special intensity. In the few seconds he had left, Halvorsen thought he saw something else there, in addition to the ferocity. Something the other beasts here didn't share. Something like reasoning...like a deep intelligence.

For a few more seconds, the huge charcoal wolf burned holes through Halvorsen with its glowing eyes. Halvorsen, for just a moment, forgot about the other wolves. He forgot about his loyal dog Valiant. The stare of this dark creature locked him in place; he wasn't sure why, and would never have time to consider it.

The dark wolf emitted a deep sound, a rumble, then the start of a howl. Merely the whiny beginning of the classic wolf call, opening its jaws just enough to show its oversized lower fangs clearly. Then it went silent, still staring into Halvorsen's eyes.

The pack surged into action, closing in uncanny unison on Halvorsen and his dog, like a fur-covered noose ringed with hungry white teeth. Halvorsen directed the shotgun to the wolf that arrived first and squeezed the trigger.

Once.

Two

Lee Bodkin walked from the kitchen and turned the corner, finding a sleepy face peering his way. His own face looked back, suddenly awestruck.

The contrast was sharp between the countenance of each: Bodkin's mug weathered, beat up and wind burned, with some subtle but permanent swelling over each brow bone. An ear touched with cauliflower scarring rested on either side of the blocky head. Too many collisions with fists and wrestling mats. But, hey, you should have seen the other guys, Bodkin often figured. His head was covered with short brown hair, if only partially. Buzzed close to the scalp, down to sandpaper length, at least where the hair still sprouted.

Conversely, the woman's face he now gazed upon was smooth instead of rough, tapered instead of square-jawed. Softness instead of roughness, protected instead of abused, influenced by sensible, planned exercise done indoors under controlled conditions. Versus his, the result of years of being subjected to life-threatening quests carried out in all manner of weather, with too much cold, heat, wind, and excessive sun. She was olive-skinned by birth; he was tan in the summer, pink in the winter. Dark hair, matching deep brown eyes, flowed over one of her shoulders and down onto the pillow case. The eyes looked into Bodkin's.

And sure enough, the womanly allure did its trick. Again. Bodkin, as usual, started to become entranced. But remembering his strategy, he snapped out of it, assuming his air of confidence. His act. Standing there in his light blue boxer shorts and nothing else, Bodkin began his approach. Still half-asleep himself, but he did his saunter as best possible. The magnetic Casanova treating the eager maiden with his presence. Um. Nice self-talk, he knew, even as he was brought in by the brunette's gravitational pull.

Lita Catalfa reached up and took his hand, pulling him down to her, like a sleek mink reeling in a gorilla. Bodkin's years of grappling paid off: upon rolling across the bed, he avoided crushing her.

This was supposed to happen last night, but...he'd conked out on her. Not his fault really, finishing a trying assignment as he had just a couple of days earlier. And the wine, the late hour, the huge dinner at the Roaring Oven Cafe. The cold temps. He was running out of excuses; now he had some catching up to do.

Well, this morning should work out in that regard, Bodkin thought. He wasn't heading out of town until 11 AM or so. Should be enough time to settle into things and not rush off. And Lita's nightwear, some peach-colored silk number, didn't appear to be a major challenge to get past. She'd give him instructions and encouragement if needed. The exploration and otherworldly sensations commenced.

But, alas...six minutes later, his cell phone, sitting on Lita's dresser, vibrated. The phone was never set to ring, but even the echo of it shaking could be bad news. However, no matter what the call concerned, it was definitely not news that would be received right now. Bad news could wait. It would wait.

But it couldn't wait. The phone issued two vibration cycles, then stopped. Oh no, thought Bodkin. Next will be one vibration, then it will again go silent. And it indeed did. Then the dreaded 10-count, after which the phone whirred back to life, the caller on the other end hanging on until he picked up. The calls with their exact ring-and-hang up pattern would only be coming from one person, and urgency, the kind you dropped everything for, the only reason. Under no conditions did false alarms occur between Bodkin and his partner. His business partner that is, not his romantic love partner. Not the one with him now, the one he would soon disappoint.

Bodkin ran his hand along Lita's arm, his look of dazed euphoria changing to one of apology. He gestured with his head toward the impatient phone as it hummed.

"I know," Lita said, attempting a smile. She flopped her head back on the pillow as Bodkin rose from the bed and took some dizzy steps to the dresser.

"Yo," Bodkin said into the phone.

"*Con il tuo amante?*" asked the female voice on the other end. *With your lover?*

"Uh, that would be a yes."

"Her place or yours?"

"Hers."

"Currently in the act?"

"None of your business, Blondie."

"Inopportune time, I gather."

"What makes you say that?" Bodkin said.

"The thickness in your voice. You finally sound like someone I want to talk to," Gladdis Montrose said.

Bodkin would have to remember that in the future, for interviewing female suspects perhaps. Use the current voice to persuade. If his eye contact – his normal mode, not the kind he made in his amorous bumbling – didn't work. Although it usually did. More to unnerve than to charm, but so far it seemed effective.

"Tell Lita I'm sorry. Obviously, something has come up," Montrose said.

"I gathered as much. Do I get to find out now?" Bodkin said.

"Certainly do. To begin with, we have to leave earlier. As soon as you can get ready, guy. Looking like this is going to be more than a simple pest eradication," Montrose said.

Bodkin was curious, but figured he knew what was next. The folks up north, in the little town on the shore of icy Lake Superior, were getting antsy. Or maybe even panicked. A wolf problem, they'd said; deer and livestock being wiped out. Even the few moose that roamed the area appeared to be gone. Last night or this morning, Bodkin predicted, another cow or horse, or group of deer, had been massacred. And the locals needed Gladdis and him up there to address it. Now. As if arriving three hours sooner would matter.

"Please continue," Bodkin said.

"The sheriff's office up in Oxide County tried to get ahold of you earlier this morning; said you didn't answer. Now I can see why."

"You overestimate my virility," Bodkin said. He looked at Lita and winked after he said it. Gotta prevent any wrong ideas from manifesting here. "I was sound asleep less than a half hour ago. So, Oxide County was looking for me. I thought the cops in Taconite Bluff were organizing the assignment," Bodkin said.

"Our paycheck gets disbursed through the county system, so the sheriff's department is in on it. Throwing their weight around. But...what they said wasn't real comforting," Montrose said.

"I'll guess. The rogue wolves are taking over the town," Bodkin said. This is what he was drawn away from his Italian lovely for?

"The pack may have taken the first step in that direction," Montrose said.

Silence entered their conversation for a moment. Gladdis trying to be funny? That didn't happen much;

and now she sounded serious, although unconcerned. Just the facts. She left the emotions and attempts at humor to Bodkin.

"Coming after pets in town now?" Bodkin said.

"Well, not all the way into the city limits. Yet. But a local townie, one of the city council guys as a matter of fact, went missing. An older guy, about 60."

"Still gone?"

"No. Eventually they determined that they'd found him," Montrose said.

Was Ms. Montrose short on sleep or something? What's with the speaking in riddles?

"Kind of a weird way to put it. 'Determined'?" said Bodkin.

"At first they couldn't tell," Montrose said.

More silence. But her statement cut through the ambiguity. A victim badly mauled at a minimum. Eaten?

"Don't tell me they consumed parts of him."

"Oh yeah. If what the deputy said was true," Montrose said.

Bodkin knew wolves as maneaters, at least in North America, were rare. So rare it was hardly considered a risk. Almost unthinkable.

"I wonder if the fellow had a heart attack or some other kind of accident. Perhaps the canines scented him out after he collapsed. It's winter after all. Starving or desperate maybe?" Bodkin said.

"Not according to what they told me. I said the same thing to the deputy on the phone, and he said no way. This gentleman, a Mr. Halvorsen, was definitely killed. And yes, by wolves."

"Was he a farmer? If so, maybe he was defending his livestock."

"No, not a farmer. He'd actually headed out for a grouse hunt."

"So he was armed with a shotgun," Bodkin said.

"Uh huh. And it wasn't enough," Montrose said.

"This pack is more ambitious than originally thought."

"I'd say. The critters are shaping up to be a bit more than a handful of mischievous coyotes," Montrose said.

"I'm not worried. Why the hurried departure? We can't save the Halvorsen guy at this point."

"Another two are missing. A couple of teens. Rock climbing guys."

This whole situation was taking an unexpected turn. And they hadn't even started the assignment yet.

"Tourists?" Bodkin said.

"Nope, locals. Dependable types, I was told. Never came back last night from what was usually a quick practice session up in the hills above town."

A small dispersal of fight-or-flight hormone started to circulate in Bodkin's system. Displacing the other more comforting chemicals from just moments ago. A different kind of arousal.

"Did the cops up there look into it?"

"They reportedly did. But as you know, there are only four town cops total, and only two of them are capable of navigating the rugged terrain. They've found nobody yet; lots of wolf tracks though."

"Thus the immediate need for our helpful ferocity," Bodkin said. "They want us to come up there and hit the ground running."

"Exactly. Ready to roll? Or you need more beauty sleep?"

"Wide awake now," Bodkin said. He turned to look again at Lita; she'd turned away onto her side by then, however. She figured she might as well keep resting. Lita knew when he and Gladdis talked shop like this, a logical next step followed. He'd be leaving.

Three

Four hours and thirteen minutes later, Gladdis Montrose looked out the window of Bodkin's truck. Through dense walls of pine and birch trees, she watched as glimpses of Lake Superior flashed by. Glistening snowdrifts blanketed the base of the trees and the shore's boulders beyond, gentle pillows of ice-cold fluff. In contrast, the snow that had landed near the waterline's crashing waves was now melted down into shiny solid ice heaps. Montrose reached her arm to her opposite shoulder after feeling long, furry jaws settle there. She stroked her hand across soft, yellow canine fur, as the dog craned forward from the truck's backseat.

"You in the mood for some exercise, girl?" she said to Sheba, who nuzzled her face further into the stroking hand. "Better be; you'll surely be getting some."

"It should be an adventure for her. She'll flush them, I'll pop whatever wolves I can from up close with buckshot, and you pick off the ones still visible in the distance. Reload and repeat, until Wolf Exhibit A is subdued and reclaimed by Mother Earth," Bodkin said from the driver's seat.

"You make it sound easy," Montrose said.

"It'll be grueling, but I picture it going like clockwork. Wolves are predictable," Bodkin said.

"Sounds like these ones aren't."

"Looking that way, I know. Unusual situation. Maneating bears, sometimes. Maneating tigers, more often. Crocodiles, any chance they get. But wolves?" Bodkin said.

"Maneating wolf is almost a contradiction in terms," Montrose said.

"Doesn't happen much. However, if this group is doing just that, we'll address the problem."

"Of course, finding those teenagers will be our first priority," Montrose said.

"Of course. Although finding them and the gathering of wolves may be the same pursuit. Sadly," Bodkin said. Montrose knew what he meant; if their worst fears were confirmed, the wolfpack may still be picking over the remains of new victims.

"Sad for a magnificent animal, too," Montrose said.

"No doubt," Bodkin said. "Hard to say what caused this supposed attack on the victim, Mr. Halvorsen. Providing it actually went down as reports suggest. If it is true, and they're prone to crunching people, these wolves go down. All of them."

"Yep. Ironic though. We'll exterminate the pack if they kill people. But over the years, the rogue predators we've been hired to catch and control, and sometimes kill, have almost always been other people," Montrose said.

"Yes. But they were all bad," Bodkin said, looking at her with a grin. Montrose smirked back, the sun from the lake sparkling off blue eyes and bright hair. She looked again at Sheba, the attention hound, continuing to fluff the fair hair on the dog's head. Sheba had her mouth open in appreciation, tongue lolled out and long, white fangs glimmering. Ready to hunt and bite wolf flesh. Capably equipped for the task: she was partly wolf herself.

Earlier they'd rocketed up the freeway from the St. Paul-Minneapolis metro area. Bodkin had – reluctantly – left Lita's apartment in St. Paul's affluent Crocus Hill neighborhood, not far from the governor's mansion and the Minnesota State Capitol. From there, just over 30 miles to the much less tony region where his house sat, in that transition land where suburbia turns to country. In particular, where the swamps started. His house rested in a marshland with sandy dirt roads snaking through it, the only houses for miles in similar isolation to his, in the trees and water-drenched weeds.

Gladdis Montrose's house, in contrast to Bodkin's, made the suburban-to-country transition with more splendor. It rested on the banks of the picturesque St. Croix River, a richly forested stretch of water designated by the federal government as wild and scenic. She'd purchased the house and land while barely able to afford it. Since then, in the years when its value didn't remain the same, it went up. And up. She could presently sell, live frugally, and never need to work again. Bodkin's property had appreciated over time too, but slowly. It didn't matter much; it would truly be a hard sell. Few people moved to his location, because few people want to live in a swamp.

Their living choices matched up well with each, the housing reflecting specific personalities. Utilitarian versus upscale. Crude versus refined. Practical versus precise.

But that's where their differences ended, and similarities began. Both Bodkin and Montrose were weapons experts, shooting enthusiasts, trackers, rescuers, and sometimes killers, neo-law enforcement specialists with bounty hunting licenses. Amazing what that license allowed you to do in the United States: much more leeway permitted than an official cop ever had.

On top of it all, they shared the love of wilderness, with its sights, sounds, and smells. Its trees, brush, density, and unpredictability. And especially its water, both choosing to live their lives right by it. Near water sources that seemed endless.

But after arriving near their assignment's destination, both Bodkin and Montrose once again felt a familiar sensation: relatively speaking, their local bodies of water didn't amount to much. The magnificent river on which Montrose lived, as well as the sprawling wetland where Bodkin hunkered down, now seemed miniscule in comparison to the lake next to which they drove. The gargantuan pool known as Lake Superior made both of those other water sources look like liquid vapor. Looking at it, and taking in its immensity, was humbling.

Lake Superior is the largest freshwater lake in the world. At its furthest points, it sprawls 350 miles long and 160 miles wide. The vast, ice-cold inland ocean reaches down over 700 feet in its deepest section. Superior's nearly constant temperature of 36°F makes it deadly for swimmers, as well as for anyone else who falls in and can't get back out. Quickly.

The big lake connects to the rest of the Great Lakes, and from there links to the Atlantic Ocean via the St. Lawrence Seaway. It is thus a crucial shipping route, allowing product from the Midwest to get to the rest of the world, and for the region to receive goods from the outside in return. This means ship traffic, and plenty of it.

Not every ship has made it. With its frigid and violent waters, safety is never guaranteed while traversing Lake Superior. Some vessels – actually many of them – have been destroyed and sunk. And the ships that have gone down rarely have portions recovered; the sailors on them are found even more rarely. Both Bodkin and Montrose knew the lore since they were kids, but the knowledge of the indescribable force contained in Lake Superior was enough to regenerate awe. Again, humbling.

The vehicle neared its destination. They'd navigated up Interstate 35, and Bodkin's truck never slowed until reaching the freeway's northern endpoint: the city of

Duluth. The historic Minnesota port town's structure displayed some chips, cracks, wear and tear, its original red brick buildings now faded, the onslaught of age and over 150 years of subzero winters. Despite this, Duluth was still a key player amongst international shipping hubs, moving loads of bulk material to the tune of 40 million tons each year. Modern Duluth was defined by little glamour but endless activity and efficiency.

Bodkin maneuvered his F-150 off the interstate and through Duluth's hardscrabble city streets, then hooked up with State Highway 61 when leaving the city. Highway 61 continued next to the giant lake, and could bring a person all the way up through northern Minnesota to the border and into Canada, if so desired.

They'd not be going that far today, however. Just 37 minutes later they arrived in the small town that had hired them and their guns. A town with a new threat lurking in the hills above it. Population 8,247; days earlier, it had been 8,248. A place with more than a few frightened residents, and one whose tiny police department awaited the arrival of the old but finely-tuned pickup truck. A truck bringing weapons handled by owners who knew how to use them, and often did. Trackers who could do their thing for days, and often did. Guided by a tracking animal, part wolf and part wolf-hunting dog, reputed to have the training to kill on command. Information of their signing up to help was received eagerly by cops and town volunteers, people who had to find two missing teens among the snowy and rugged terrain, but were now afraid to try. Folks who had recently recovered the remains of one of their neighbors, a lifelong resident and council member of the town, who had no longer been physically intact when found. They needed help, and help had now arrived.

Lee Bodkin knew about threats, and he knew about

danger. He also knew about wild predators; although the task ahead would be exhausting, Bodkin figured it would be routine. He was wrong. Gladdis Montrose sensed he was underestimating their quarry, and she was right. Neither felt fear about what awaited them, but they should have.

The trio rode along Highway 61 to exit 920, then steered off the highway. They veered even closer to the lakeshore, and approached the ancient steel bridge that crosses the Maelstrom River. Clunking across the rusty bridge, Bodkin and Montrose looked out either side of the vehicle, glimpsing the river's gushing, fertile water, loaded with minerals and brown from its iron content. The water resembled root beer, the froth atop its eddies and whirlpools like matching root beer foam. The river was deep in some spots, shallow in others, lined with gnarly, jagged stone walls everywhere. They could see mist from Maelstrom Falls, where the river dropped just over 30 feet to continuing jagged, aggressive rocks below, right before it emptied into Lake Superior.

Safer sections of the Maelstrom were popular for swimming during hot summer weather. Both Bodkin and Montrose had fished trout in it a few times, but neither had ever gone swimming in it. That was about to change.

In another two minutes, the truck rolled down the small and quiet main street of Taconite Bluff, Minnesota.

Four

"Rob Waverly," said the husky police chief. Bodkin figured him to be about mid-50s, easy going and inactive, more of an in-town type of officer. The kind who avoided, if possible, the rigors of the outdoors. Bodkin guessed, in contrast, that the two cops standing on either side of him were not.

"And this is Officer Cora Rutherford," Waverly said, turning toward the female cop on his right. About 30, light brown hair tied back in a bun, lean physique, one thumb in her service pistol's holster belt, the other hand hanging loose and open. Ready. Standing straight and proud, gaze calm and steady as she appraised the two new arrivals. A Gladdis Montrose type, thought Bodkin. *Great, I'll be working with two of them.* She was maybe an inch or so taller than Montrose, but still on the petite side. And like Montrose, she looked strong. Physically, and also from an intangible aura of fortitude, visible in her eyes.

Of course, on second thought, having a carbon copy of Gladdis along might not be the worst thing, Bodkin knew. Montrose could direct high-powered bullets into exact places, from afar and through tight places. She was a nationally ranked biathlete, and thus had plenty of practice shooting while exhausted: perfect for this particular job. Plus, Montrose didn't just blast away; she hit targets. With a precision Bodkin could never acquire, despite all his weaponry drills. Almost no one could develop that kind of exactness for bull's-eyes, truth be told. Not even the many ex-military and government agents Bodkin had come into contact with and worked beside.

Montrose was gutsy, courageous but not stupid. Nothing superficial to prove; she knew when to fight, and when to run. Considering the focus of the assignment – maneating wolves – maybe another Gladdis type wouldn't be so bad after all. Time would tell if the lady cop here was in the same league. She had the attitude down, if nothing else.

Standing on the ice-glazed sidewalk in front of the police station, the five of them felt the breeze from the lake let up for a moment. The reprieve allowed the early afternoon weather to give the full comfort only 11°F can deliver. At least it was above zero, for now.

"And this is Lieutenant Frank Wells," Waverly said.

Bodkin looked from Cora Rutherford to Lieutenant Wells. Maybe late 40s, max, and possessed of a contained energy, similar to his much smaller lady partner. He had an experienced, tough, and world-weary look about his face, but Bodkin made a quick observation that his brow and ears were not sporting scar tissue, and his nose had been assaulted little if at all. Unlike the face and head of Bodkin, bearing the wrestling and fighting scars permanently. This Wells guy was probably too intelligent and had too much sense to burn up his body, face, and youth like that. As Bodkin had. Besides, in this part of the U.S. and up into nearby sections of Canada, commerce mostly consisted of mining, lumber, shipping, fishing, and one very big, very cold lake. And the resulting cave-ins, accidents, explosions, drownings, and catastrophes that go along with such work and settings. Considering the natural challenges settlers in these parts faced over the last 200 years, and the Native Americans before them for time immemorial, squaring off with some guy to engage in a fistfight seemed a little, well, anticlimactic. Bodkin knew that now, at his age; he'd just been one of many tough guys who'd been slow to catch on.

"Lee Bodkin; and this is my partner and quality control specialist Gladdis Montrose," Bodkin said, and handshakes were exchanged.

"Quality control how?" Wells said. He looked back at Bodkin, remaining perfectly neutral.

Kind of lacking a sense of humor, Bodkin thought. "She sees to it that things are killed on a precise and regular schedule," Bodkin replied. Hey, it was an attempt at humor. Wells wasn't buying it.

"So she's good at it?" Wells said, looking over at Montrose, evaluating.

"We'll have to see," Montrose said back. "I've done OK in the past."

"Then we'll need your skills," Wells said.

Waverly interrupted. "We'll introduce you to Mancheski later. He's the fourth and final member of our department. His shift ended a while ago, but he's hanging around inside still. A neighbor dropped off a dozen donuts earlier, to help with the effort. He should be on his third donut by now."

"Isn't he saving any for the rest of you?" Bodkin said.

"I already had a couple; thanks for your concern," Waverly said.

"I'd definitely be willing to help out if he's having trouble finishing them. You had any?" Bodkin said, looking at Rutherford.

She hesitated at first, awakening from her state of serious concentration. "Uh, yeah, I had one," she replied, peering at Wells with a quizzical look.

"You?" Bodkin said, now turning to Wells.

Wells ignored Bodkin's comment. "Pull your truck up at the end of Main Street just over an hour from now. Cora and I will meet you there; we'll take the department's Land Rover. We'll go down a logging road about a half-mile, then leave the vehicles there. Your rig can handle an unplowed road?"

"We're good to go," Bodkin said.

"No hot-rodding though; it's an unmaintained stretch," Wells said.

"Lucky I'm driving, in that case," Bodkin said, looking over at Montrose, a subtle accusation being implied. Montrose started to smirk, but recovered into an even-keeled expression. One of them had to appear the professional.

"You two will go high, along a ridge overlooking the Maelstrom River. The two of us will be heading down along the river. So we as a group will cover both areas as we search for the kids. Plus, if the wolves are hanging in the lower areas, we may drive some up to you. If any of the pack is spotted up top where you're searching, you can have at them. Either way, do your thing right away. Shoot any wolves on sight."

"Could there be any wolves around who are not problem specimens?" Bodkin asked.

"Doubtful. All the native wolves, genuine timber wolves, seem to have disappeared. We think these new ones, bigger ones, killed them off."

"You see any of these larger beasts yet?" Montrose said.

"Yep, we have one's carcass. Big and bulky, hard to believe it's a regular wolf."

"And there's evidence of plenty more out there still?" Bodkin said.

"Hell yes. The amount of big tracks around the kill sight was not typical. A very big pack."

"You've definitely got our interest. OK, meet you in an hour," Bodkin said.

"Bring your A-game, folks," said Cora Rutherford.

"You haven't seen what we have."

"We're not too worried," Bodkin said.

"Then let me pass on this little story," said Wells. "We went up to recover the body of Chuck Halvorsen, the man who was recently killed. We thought we'd need to hire some of the cannery workers and a dock guy or two to help with the carry, but it wasn't needed. Just Cora and I carried the bag back down to town. It was that light."

Bodkin stayed quiet, letting any witty attitude dissipate. The last statement Wells had made created an impression. Not much left of their neighbor to transport, remains sparse enough to carry with ease. Oh man. Explained their lack of humor, pretty much.

Chief Waverly broke the awkward silence. "For a second there I thought you'd captured one of the wolves and brought it with you," Waverly said, looking over at Sheba. The dog peered from the back window of the F-150, eyes steady and intense, elongated jaws clamped shut and ready. "What kind of beast you got in there?"

"One you'd definitely not want tracking you down," Bodkin said, and he and Montrose turned and went to his truck.

Five

"What exactly is your plan here, Bodkin?" asked Montrose.

"Double duty," Bodkin said. "I don't think we'll be in town that long. Get the job done and get out of here. So I brought a prototype of my new bow."

For the other half of his income Bodkin crafted historic archery equipment, mainly longbows. They were a weapon whose design and use dated back thousands of years, and with the arrows fired from them were able to harvest heavy, burly animals like black bears and deer. And sometimes even larger game. Bodkin sold many of his handcrafted bows to both hunters and historical weapons hobbyists. But even more longbows were purchased by a segment other than those groups, specifically by the target archery competitors throughout North America. Hundreds of archers competed in traditional equipment leagues in the U.S. It was almost a secret society, and one that yearned for whatever new and better products it could get its hands on. Healthy profits awaited those who could give these target archers the weapons they wanted.

Bodkin planned to meet up with a man here in town who was one of the archery community's most influential competitors and organizers. One who could get Bodkin's wooden archery marvels in front of a hungry new group of buyers. Problem was, that guy was also someone who didn't much like seeing Bodkin around. They went back a ways.

At the bed of his truck, Bodkin undid a tarp snapped down in several spots. He lifted the tarp aside, and reached over to a lockbox just behind the truck's cab. He dialed the combination on its lock, popped it open, and from the compartment withdrew a long cardboard container, the glimmering new longbow encased within it.

"I need to expand my market; both this part of the Midwest and Ontario are big on traditional archery. Mickey just might be the key to it. My meal ticket."

"We have time for this?"

"We'll just say hello, let him know about the new product," Bodkin said.

"Aren't you two still on bad terms?" Montrose said.

"Yes. But we always are," Bodkin said. "Let's go."

With some reluctance, Montrose walked along with Bodkin, his boxed-up bow under one arm. They wandered in the direction of the Wild Rice Cafe, Mickey Manoomin's headquarters.

***

The cafe vibrated with the noise of coffee cups, spoons, forks, and opinions. Smells of warm toast, sizzling eggs, and salty ham slices wafted throughout, and a small group of employees maneuvered and scurried around. Occupied with the cafe's abundant food: searing it, flipping it, and carrying it.

"Look what the cat dragged in," said Mickey Manoomin, standing from his stool behind the counter. He stood about 6'3", three inches and a millimeter taller than Bodkin, and more than a foot above Montrose. Mickey was American Indian of an Ojibwe and Sioux mixture, and used some of his traditional cultural knowledge in the worlds of archery and canoe building. But the main focus of his life was his circle of cronies, his wife, the big lake, and his rustic restaurant. The Wild Rice Cafe served as a major food source for truckers going to and from Canada along Highway 61, and was operated always with a keen eye on profits. Like now.

"What'll you folks have?" Mickey said.

"You haven't seen me for almost a year and that's what you open the conversation with?" Bodkin said.

"I run a business here. It's either buy or bye."

"Of course, Mickey. But first...I have a business proposition you may be interested in," Bodkin said.

"No," Mickey said.

"Yes, I think, once you hear me out. You're still the commissioner of the Northern Archers Association, right?"

"Assistant commissioner."

"That sounds just as good. I think you'd be in a great position to help me spread the word on my archery products. Especially a new model I came up with," Bodkin said. "Triple-laminated limbs on this particular new longbow. Hickory, bamboo, and yew wood. Your promotional help could be profitable for both of us."

"There's an ancient Sioux expression used when a cheapskate tries to talk you into a deal," Mickey said.

"Oh? What's the expression?" Bodkin asked.

"Too polite to say in here," Mickey said.

"Who's the cheapskate?" Bodkin said.

At that, Mickey and Montrose exchange knowing glances.

"I'm simply shrewd, that's all," Bodkin said, in his defense. "You've got a rep as pretty tight yourself, Mickey."

Mickey studied Bodkin said. "Is this your way of angling for free coffee?"

"Well, we *are* newly arrived guests in town," Bodkin said. He gave Mickey a sprightly smile, making his beaten face and perpetually aggressive expression suddenly look...kind of amusing.

"You both like it black, if I remember," Mickey said, relenting and turning to the brewing station. A moment later two steaming mugs appeared on the counter in front of them.

"Yep, no cream or sugar for either of us anymore," Bodkin said. "I've got her trained." He could hear Montrose let out a slight sigh of exasperation next to him.

"Oh, really?" Mickey said. "I remember the first year you two worked together, she pretty much had you at her beck and call."

"I was single then," Bodkin said. "Anyway, thanks for the java. The boost will help us kick off the big snow safari for the mythical killer beasts."

Mickey's countenance changed a little, the adversarial banter draining from it. "You're heading out there today?"

"Yeah. In minutes, actually."

"And you stop off to make a business deal first?"

"No time like the present."

"You seem to be taking the expedition a little lightly, Bodkin," Mickey said.

"We're in top condition currently. What's to worry about?" Bodkin said.

"Well, you were called here because of the missing teens, right? Those two kids are tough and agile, and not daredevils either."

"We'll find them," Bodkin said.

"I hope you like what you find. I'd help, but I just can't hack it anymore out there. Too rugged. And you heard about Halvorsen," Mickey said.

"Yes. Not good."

"No. And it gets worse. Remember wild man Burt Langbein?" Mickey said.

"A little bit. Heard things about him, saw him down

by the river over the years when I've been fishing."

"Yep, he set up his otter traps down there, and along just about every creek in the area for mink. He used to, at least."

Bodkin and Montrose now both looked at Mickey, waiting.

"No one has seen him for two months. He always wandered around armed, too. With both a .22 revolver and a big .45 Colt. You'd think he'd be safe from attack. Halvorsen was a hunter, but Langbein had more the instinct of a predator. He was in the woods more than in town. Hunted everything that moved since he was seven years old or so. If he got taken down, those instincts and guns didn't matter. That says something."

"Maybe he got injured and couldn't make it out on his own," Montrose said.

"Maybe. Anyway, last time I'd talked to him, he said the trapping was terrible. Rabbits, mink, otters, suddenly all sparse. But he mentioned something more disturbing," Mickey said.

They waited some more, saying nothing. Mickey continued.

"Area wolves, ones up in the hills and along the river where he trapped, have been preyed upon; the original ones, that is, local timber wolves. Langbein had found two timber wolf carcasses at the end of last summer; not much left of them," Mickey said. "The other members of the local pack seemed to be missing. As if they'd migrated from the area completely."

"Animals often move on," Bodkin offered. He had the first tingling of a strange feeling, one suggesting perhaps there was more to this assignment than first thought.

"But why? All of a sudden they leave? Some of the local packs have bred and lived in these parts for the last thousand years or more," Mickey said.

"So what do you think? Any ideas?" Montrose said.

"A gang of werewolves, maybe? That's almost what it seems like. Two of our cops, Cora and Frank, found tons of wolf tracks. Normal prints, except for their unusually large size. And exceptional for the sheer number of them that are running out there someplace," Mickey said. "You two bringing along some capable weaponry?"

"The usual. A shotgun and a sniper rifle."

"AK-47s might be a better idea," Mickey said. "Got backup besides those hunting arms?"

"I carry a sidearm," Montrose said.

"She's a pistolier now, Mickey. You'd be amazed," Bodkin said.

"Yeah, I heard a little about the Twin Cities Marathon attack on the governor. You took out, what, a dozen of the bad guys with your handgun?" Mickey asked Montrose.

"Not that many. Stories get blown out of proportion," Montrose said.

"Good work, in any case. How about you, tough guy. Carrying backup?" Mickey asked Bodkin.

"Of course," Bodkin said.

"Same handgun as your lovely partner here?"

"I'm not much of a handgun man, but I carry one. For a paper weight, mainly."

"What kind?" Mickey asked.

"You don't need specifics," Bodkin said.

"I don't need interruptions in my cafe either," Mickey said. "Which is what you are. I'm only asking, because I'm afraid you might have too little ammunition on your person."

"We'll stop at a jewelry store down in Duluth first and pick up some silver pieces. How's that sound?"

Bodkin said.

"What?"

"To coat the bullets. For the werewolves," Bodkin said.

"How do you remain partners with this boy?" Mickey asked Montrose.

Mickey then looked for an instant down the counter, at the row of customers sitting there. A couple of truck drivers remained, finishing lunch, plus some locals who had just settled in, on break from the fish cannery down the road. He turned back to Bodkin and Montrose.

"You working with a trio of federal agents on this wolf thing? Or is it just the two of you?" Mickey said, with his voice now lowered.

"Just us," Montrose said, her tone also subdued. Both she and Bodkin harbored quizzical thoughts, but after Mickey perused the crowd in the cafe before asking, the two of them maintained poker faces. Waiting.

Mickey said a few words to his short-order cook and the waitress near him, gesturing with his head to the yard in back. The waitress nodded, then Mickey turned back to Montrose and Bodkin. "Come on outside. I'll show you my most recent canoe."

A minute later the three of them stood out in the yard, about 200 feet from the cafe and Mickey's adjoining house. The breeze came in a sudden gust off Lake Superior, delivering a wind chill sensation on their skin equivalent to -6°F. Then the breeze subsided, and the temp soared back up: all the way to 10°F above. Cozy.

"Here's my latest," Mickey said, pulling the snow-dusted covering off a canoe next to his old shed. "Think making one of your longbows is a task, Bodkin?"

The canoe Mickey had built was a full 21-footer, a little longer and a little wider than the typical canoe.

Those smaller models were purchased and used for standard purposes, like normal rivers and calm lakes. Not this one. Handcrafted and made of birchbark, the vessel was specially designed to handle big water. Actually, the biggest and least forgiving water around. The lake on whose shore it now rested. They took in the sight of its birch material beauty, its size, and the perfection with which it was created.

"Took 15 months to build," Mickey said.

"It's beautiful, Mickey," Montrose said.

"Thanks, miss. I'm glad you think so, because this is my last one."

"Bringing it to market?" Bodkin asked.

"Nah, I'm done selling them. I'm too old to keep this up. My wrists and hands are getting worn, maybe arthritis setting in," Mickey said. "Back gets sore doing woodwork now too. Nope, this canoe is my last. And I made it for myself. For navigating the cold waves out there."

Bodkin wondered for a moment what kind of skill and nerve it would take to canoe on that big, treacherous water. Full-size ships had been conquered by Lake Superior; he'd rather not learn firsthand what canoeing on it would feel like.

He noticed Mickey had run a dense length of chain through the components of the craft, and secured them with a heavy padlock. Smart. No sense letting your prized creation, especially one you took over a year to finish, walk off with thieving, undeserving new owners.

"Anyway, I like it, but it's just a canoe. Before I become hypothermic, I needed to mention something to you two," Mickey said, hugging long arms over a wide chest; he wore but a flannel shirt on his upper body. "You said you aren't coordinating the wolf-hunting efforts here with any Feds."

"No, there are no Feds teaming up with us. Funny you should suggest it," Bodkin said.

"I suggest it because some of them are in town, for the express purpose of gathering information on the wolfpack. And helping with the problem in general, I guess."

"In town?" Bodkin said.

"Yep. Three of them," Mickey said.

"Who are they with?"

"They said the Bureau of Natural Materials," Mickey said.

Bodkin didn't hesitate. "There's no such agency," he said.

"You sound pretty sure of that."

"I'm positive of it. The two of us know every federal agency in existence. We've worked for almost half of them," Bodkin said.

Mickey was silent for a moment. "I thought they seemed a bit off. Only one spoke; he was the big, in-charge guy. Another one, a tall lean man, looked off in the distance. Wouldn't establish eye contact. And the third guy wouldn't break it; kept staring at me, looked to be on the verge of grinning the whole time."

This just keeps getting better.

"They told Rob Waverly, he's the chief here – " Mickey said.

"Just met him," Bodkin interrupted.

"Yeah, good. Told him to keep the three of them updated on any wolfpack developments. Said it was federal government priority, whatever that means."

"Where are they now?"

"Staying in the Maxitel Suites, four blocks down from here. Came in late last night, driving a nondescript white minivan. Windows completely smoked," Mickey said. "The Oxide County Sheriff's Department called

Waverly as well. Requested he and his crew cooperate with the federal guys. Waverly told me Oxide County is getting some kind of pressure from above, somehow. From somewhere. And Oxide County partly subsidizes our little police force here, so..."

So they had to go along to get along. Bodkin and Montrose looked at each other for a few seconds, then Bodkin shrugged.

"Not our concern, at this point. We'll get the show on the road, find out what we can. We'll determine the pattern of the animals, intercept them and take them out. Then we'll be outta here," Bodkin said.

Mickey looked back at Bodkin, like he wanted to say more. But he didn't. He nodded to Montrose, then turned and started to walk back to the rear entrance of the cafe.

"See you tomorrow regarding the archery product launch; I think you'll like my business proposition," Bodkin said to Mickey's back. Mickey didn't turn around. Instead, he opened the door and went inside, leaving Bodkin and Montrose outside in the breeze.

The two of them walked toward the truck. Time to roll. See what kind of signs or clues could be found in the forests above, related to the supposed unstoppable threat that lurked there. Bodkin was getting tired of the drama concerning these pests. First the town council here making their emergency request, then the county sheriff's department calling over to check on what the small group of police in town were doing. Then the cops, Cora Rutherford and Frank Wells, seeming testy and actually a little afraid. Next was Mickey Manoomin, who, as far as Bodkin knew, only feared the power of nature, Lake Superior, and little else. Other things were small potatoes to him. But conversely, he seemed intimidated somehow about the wolf situation. And now...now...Gladdis next to him seemed ill at ease. What the hell was going on here?

"You seem kind of on edge. What's going on?" Bodkin said.

"Dude. Even Mickey suggests caution regarding the predators up in the hills. Should we wait until we know more, and have a more strategic attack plan here?"

"The 'predators up in the hills'? Please. Nothing more than rogue wolves, basically just oversized coyotes. We've faced much worse before. Trust me, Gladdis my dear. It'll be routine."

Six

Predators up in the hills? Yes. Routine? No.

Lee Bodkin had owned the shotgun most of his adult life. It was about to be plunged into a frigid river, deep and swirling, never to be recovered. He'd maintained the gun with impeccable care the entire time he'd used it, and the gun had always performed with precision. It did just a moment ago, for example, anchoring and killing four giant wolves, three of them instantly with the first shot. He'd wasted eight shells, however, as the canine attackers stayed in constant motion and blended into the brush, somehow staying behind cover. Concealing themselves, at least partly, until their final rush at him on the right, or Gladdis Montrose on the left, or Sheba, in the center of their makeshift formation.

Every few moments, a distinct and short howl-and-growl combination would sound from the dense brush, and the wolves would then send one of their group out into the open, looking for blood. That animal would quickly be shot down. But after each shot, more wolves would arrive, and another one or two would sprint in for the kill. All following that distinct howl-growl, different from the sounds most of the wolves made.

The attacks couldn't go on forever: one would get through and maul them. Or all of the attackers would.

Montrose had dropped four of the pack herself, but clear shots through the thick stuff were challenging at best. One tiny twig getting in the way of her .243-caliber sniper slug could mean the bullet flying up, down, or sideways, and off the mark. Spent shells from both her rifle and Bodkin's 12-gauge littered the snowy rock floor at their feet. They'd soon be out of ammunition at the rate they were shooting. And missing. The targets moved with such frantic – almost strategic – maneuvers, that the lead flying from their guns mostly found dead air. Montrose worked the bolt action on her weapon with instant and effortless efficiency, bringing the iron sight bead on one wolfen target after another, until they'd float behind brushy protection. She'd brought four rifle magazines, each holding four long, pointy shells; she had just fed the last one into her weapon. Two bursts had been used from that reload, meaning two bullets left.

The attack had been so fast, Bodkin and Montrose could barely get their guns up to meet the first charge. The team of three had just climbed to the highest point they could see while trudging along the ridge above the Maelstrom River. A massive bluff, one which jutted up then way out, its edge balancing above a deep and violent section of the river, 70 feet below. They were going to use the bluff's highest spot as an overlook, just their initial stage of the scouting mission. They were merely getting situated when Sheba issued a growling alarm. Visitors. Which attacked. Bodkin and Montrose attacked back, with the boom of a shotgun and the crack of a rifle.

The first two wolves sprawled dead near them, their blood expanding on the white snow, when the others showed themselves. Seemed like 10 or more at first, then 20, at least. As the wolves materialized in their creeping semicircle, Bodkin, Montrose, and Sheba had been backed up the bluff. More shooting ensued. The next couple of wolves fell, more came ahead, and then the three of them were pushed even further up...almost to the cliff's edge. Standing on not much more than the narrow stone triangle that formed the bluff's pinnacle. Every piece of solid ground down the bluff from them seemed to have a wolf crouching in the brush or scrambling through it. The growls vibrated through the air, each beast waiting for its chance to make its attack and tear into them. This was obviously, and quickly, turning out to be anything but typical. To be anything even remotely routine.

Sheba was nearly impossible to restrain; Bodkin had to shove her back with a boot several times, and other times hooked a leg across her neck to prevent her from rushing forward. She wanted to get to the enemy wolves and sink her fangs in, to protect her master and other partner. She didn't understand: a single one of these beasts would probably test all of her fighting capacities. Four or five swarming on her would be like getting dropped into a meat grinder. Each time Bodkin restrained Sheba, the wolves seemed to use the distraction and send forward another.

Sheba eventually got to use her fangs. One wolf was delayed by its confrontation with her long enough for Bodkin to swing his gun and pound a load of buckshot into its lungs. As it dropped crippled and dying in front of them, Sheba finished it with a blurring bite and shake, seizing the base of the wolf's thick neck and twisting with merciless and spastic energy. Another wolf ran forward, fangs bared, to savage Sheba as she vanquished its partner. Montrose finessed a slug into its open mouth and to the vital tissues beyond, killing it in a microsecond, its body continuing with momentum and skidding on the snow toward them. One bullet left.

"Last one, Lee," Montrose said, at medium volume but with urgency impossible to conceal. The newly slain wolf twitched just a couple of meters from her feet, steam billowing from its nostrils.

"Handgun ready to go?" Bodkin said, the barrel of his shotgun sweeping across the brush, waiting for the next fur-covered rocket to fly at them.

"Yeah, but I don't like those odds. Only nine rounds in it, no refill," Montrose said. Her rifle was up, ready to make the last shot count. No more iffy attempts could be afforded.

"Your backup piece with you?" she asked quickly.

"Yeah, but it's buried in my pack," Bodkin said. This was to be routine. Why would he need a spare armament? *Fuck.* "We gotta go."

"Only one way to go from here," Montrose said. "You serious?"

"No choice. Plus the cliff gives a straight drop to the river," Bodkin said. "I'll cover you two as you jump."

"Two?"

"Yep, you'll have to scoop up the She-Devil and jump with her. She'll be shredded up here by herself."

A wolf rushed from the cover, toward Bodkin, and Montrose popped off her last bullet through its heart. Sheba whined and went at it, and Bodkin was forced again to thrust her away and behind them.

Finally the beast giving the rest of the wolves their commands showed itself. For just an instant. The desperation in the voices of Bodkin and Montrose lured it closer perhaps, likely the smell and sense of a sure kill nearly irresistible to it.

Despite the frantic events, Bodkin's first impression was how striking the canine was in appearance. Colored much darker than the rest, not quite black, but rather a deep grey. Clearly bigger than all of the other wolves. Eyes a deep yellow, amber actually, glowing somehow with a combination of hatred, hunger, and elation. And knowing. The sight made Bodkin pause a second, then he knew this one was the key wolf to kill.

Two more wolves stalked from the density, but Bodkin shifted the bead from those to the monstrous-sized one, the newly appearing charcoal grey wolf. He pointed the shotgun at the center of its neck, when it let out a quick yipping noise. Bodkin squeezed the trigger just as one of its pack sped in front of it, and Bodkin's buckshot pounded into that second wolf's shoulder and collapsed the lungs beneath it.

"Only one shot left here, Gladdis. Grab her and go!" Bodkin yelled, glancing at Montrose as she wrapped her empty rifle's strap crossways across her body. Then he looked back at the bristling pack, now leaving the thicket's branches, sensing their adversary's weakness. Bodkin readied himself to take out one more with his final shotgun blast. After that, he'd be empty...what then? Only one thing he could do. Dive.

He heard Sheba screech in protest as she was picked up. "Come on girl!" Montrose yelled, encircling Sheba's chest with both arms and lifting, not easy as the dog was fully as big as her. Montrose backpedaled with the flailing dog, to the very edge of the cliff, flexed her legs once, and burst up, out, and into thin air. With Sheba issuing one more shriek, they plunged to the dark, deep pool far below.

Bodkin scrambled over to the edge from which Montrose had just leapt, just in time to intercept yet another set of wolf fangs headed his way. A fast and fatal blast hit that wolf as the others before it. Then the action of his old semiautomatic shotgun, like any semiautomatic once empty, stayed open. He was facing the pack, starting the last partial steps backward toward the ledge, taking a last moment to look back at them. That was all the time it took, however, for the pack leader, the big charcoal grey bastard with the glowing eyes, to make its sound. The same croaking howl sound the big alpha beast made before, the one that every other time sent a member of the pack forward for an assault. This time the growl-howl was a few seconds longer though. After issuing it, the big charcoal wolf stepped completely into the open, no longer hiding, ready to join the others in the attack.

It knew.

The action of his gun was open, a gentle wisp of gunpowder wafting from it, signaling that he was out of ammo. He didn't reach to his belt for more, as there was none left. The big grey wolf seemed like it knew the danger was gone. That wolf, and the dozen or so wolves obeying it, all rushed toward him at once.

Bodkin lunged backward off the cliff, initiating the 70-foot drop to the deep, icy, rusty brown water below, where Montrose and Sheba already swam. As he did it, the thought exploded in his mind: at the end, they'd rushed without reservation, in accordance with him having no ammunition left. With its strange, haunting growl, the big leader of the pack had let them know he was out of ammo.

It knew.

Seven

Cora Rutherford and Frank Wells stepped into Bodkin's hotel room, each carrying a rifle strapped across one shoulder. Montrose shut the door behind them as they entered, then went back into a slumped position in the armchair next to the TV set. Bodkin kept an arm looped around Sheba's neck, restraining and reassuring the dog.

"Easy girl, it's OK," Bodkin said. "They're on our side. Nice people. So nice, in fact, they may have brought us a big bottle of bourbon and cut us our paycheck already. Maybe we can now leave."

"Huh. No paycheck or whiskey, but we did bring you these," Wells said, as he and Rutherford unstrapped the guns on their shoulders and leaned them against the walls. Lever-action, no scopes. Both had an old but rarely used look to them. "Our standard department long arm, .30-30 Winchester. Familiar with lever action guns?"

Montrose nodded to him; Bodkin continued to look at Sheba, stroking her now-dried fur. A little embarrassed about what had went down, and about them losing their own weapons.

"Plus a box of 20 each," Rutherford said, withdrawing two unopened boxes of bullets from her police-issue parka and setting them on a coffee table. Sheba moved from Bodkin to her, smelling her hand, sizing her up. No fear on the dog's part; more like an evaluation.

"Some kind of slender Irish Wolfhound or something?" Rutherford said.

"Close. Russian Borzoi mix," Bodkin said.

"Ah, the Borzoi," Wells said. "Used for hunting

wolves over the centuries. What's the mix part?"

"Wolf, actually," Bodkin said.

Wells thought about that for a second, and Rutherford raised her eyebrows.

"You don't say. How fitting," Wells said. "On that subject...part of the reason you were hired up here, to find the two teens...," Wells stopped and went quiet, looking pensive. Emotional, actually. First time Bodkin and Montrose had seen it.

Bodkin completed his thought for him. "It's not looking good for them, is it?"

"No. Dwindling chances with every hour, actually. Even if no animals attacked them, the exposure to the elements overnight, for more than one night especially, would seal their doom."

"If they faced a fraction of the wolfpack we did, I think their doom was assured," Montrose said. "Lee and I have seen a lot of things at this point. The attack today, especially its coordination, was the stuff of nightmares."

"Nevertheless, we'd like to find those young men," Wells said. "Hard to do it with a hungry menace out there."

"We'll stay on board with the eradication commitment," Bodkin said. "We'll kill as many as we can, Frank. Then we'll be gone. If the boys are already dead, that gets out of our hands."

"It does. Glad you'll stay for the predators, however. You mentioned on the phone both your guns were lost in the river, so as you see, we brought the ones there. Will they hold you over for now?"

"Yep. Thanks, by the way. They should be fine. Plus, I'm ready to call in replacements," Bodkin said.

"Call in? Your operation that big?" Wells asked.

"I have a system worked out," Bodkin said.

"Any firearms at all in your possession?"

"I retained my pistol," Montrose said. "Had to part ways with the rifle while going for that swim. Just too heavy, I was going down."

Wells nodded. "The Maelstrom is a feisty river," he said. Then to Bodkin, "How about you? Carrying a pistol of some kind?"

"Yeah, but I'm not much of a handgun man," Bodkin said. "The rifles will be fine, until I get the replacement guns delivered up here at least. We'll be heading out first thing in the morning."

"You two up for it that soon?" Wells said.

"If not, we'll get ourselves up for it," Bodkin said. "We realize the desperate situation here, and we kind of blew it earlier."

"Don't be too hard on yourselves. A full wolfpack contributed to the snafu," Wells said.

"On the bright side, it's now only half a wolfpack," Montrose said.

"Really?" Wells said.

"Yeah, but there's no wiggle room if people are being killed," Bodkin said. "All of the marauders have to go. We're being more cautious this next time, needless to say. What we now know – what we learned after their onslaught – may be the key."

"Key to what?"

"Key to an unfair fight. Stacking the odds in our favor this next time," Montrose said. "We might have a surprise in store for them. Just have to do the proper recon to know if our plan is possible."

"Want to let us in on the plan?" Wells said.

"We win, they lose," Bodkin said.

"Sounds good. Specifics?" Wells said.

"Are we hired to take care of this menace, or are we simply here as your assistants?" Bodkin said.

"You're free to operate as you see fit. Just so the job

gets done," Wells said.

"Cool. We'll let you know as things develop," Bodkin said. "Again, thanks for the rifles."

"Don't mention it."

They left, Rutherford clicking the old hotel room door shut softly.

Eight

Earlier, they'd scrambled up a steep river bluff less than 50 yards from Maelstrom Falls, where the dark, chilled water dumped from the river down over layer after layer of jagged, wicked rocks below. Both strong swimmers, Bodkin and Montrose were nonetheless hindered by the frigid water temps, and barely able to help Sheba stay above water while saving themselves. No retriever was she. By using the ends of a couple of fallen trees, they managed to push the dog out of the river and onto the rocky bank just in time, then proceed to yank themselves out, continuing their life on this earth. None of them would have survived the waterfall's drop.

Once on solid ground, the three of them burst up the steep bluff. Sheba, with a thick fur coat, was in less danger now than Bodkin and Montrose. The reason: the human icicle factor. Specifically, the challenge to not become one.

Sopping wet with winds alternating between gentle and biting, the heat was being whisked from them at record speed, and the cold – deadly cold – was sinking into their bodies. Despite their current exhaustion, Bodkin and Montrose used their uncanny endurance base to do what made the most sense: sprint. And then sprint some more. Then sprint even faster.

Eleven minutes later, plowing through the front door of the age-old hotel where they were staying, the heat inside was like a giant, warm, velvet glove wrapping around them. As their lungs heaved, euphoria soaked through both of them. Partly because they were now safe, and partly because they had the first stages of hypothermia, a strange phenomenon which caresses the victim closer to death, but soothes them nevertheless.

The matronly woman at the front desk, Ethyl, maybe Esther, eyed them with a neutral look. Weird event? Maybe, but so what? She looked like she'd seen it all.

"Out fishing I bet. I heard there was a winter steelhead run in the river. Looks like they weren't cooperating," she said.

"They told us to take a flying leap," Bodkin said. The trio scampered upstairs to Bodkin's room.

***

The packaged coffee in the room wasn't top-notch, but Bodkin doubled up the dose with two bags. The dense brew was a little bitter, but strong and steamy. He and Montrose slouched in the room's antique chairs sipping it, letting their bodies come back to life, letting the shock of the attack wear off. Sheba was lying nearby on the floor and gnawed a beef bone Bodkin had packed for her. The dog was at ease and gave the impression that the recent wolf showdown had never even happened.

Then Bodkin called down to St. Paul to touch base with Lita. The call changed everything.

"Glad you're safe, babe. Don't want to hit you with this right off the bat," Lita said. "But you'll want to know."

Huh?

"When you described your current assignment earlier, something rung a bell. I was sleepy at the time, so it didn't resonate until later. I looked into some things."

"You shouldn't have."

"You know me, Lee. I had to," Lita said. "Curiosity killed the cat and all."

"Ah, yes. I definitely didn't picture you getting in on

this," Bodkin said.

"Well, I am."

"So now it's a total group effort. What'd you find?"

"OK. As you know, my firm both lends money to government agencies, and insures stuff they buy with that same money," Lita said.

"You got 'em coming and going. No wonder the U.S. is going broke," Bodkin said.

"Shelve it, Mr. Free Enterprise. Anyway. Agencies in both Ontario and Idaho have been desperate to address their disappearing moose and elk herds. Deer are taking a hit too. Due to new – and very ravenous – wolfpacks introduced into their regions."

"Sounds like we're on the same subject. I just saw some enthusiastic wolves up close recently," Bodkin said.

"You spotted some?" Lita asked.

"We almost fed them, actually," Bodkin said.

"Fed them?"

"Please go on, dear," Bodkin said.

"Yes. So of course we had to determine who was introducing these new wolf populations. Turns out the department is known as the U.S. Center for Defense Maneuvers."

"Never heard of them."

"Not well known. At the firm, our analysts can't even determine who approved their department's creation," Lita said. "Don't seem to officially exist."

"Speaking of which, my sweet. There are a few guys in town here now, looking into the wolf situation supposedly. Refer to their department as The Bureau of Natural Materials," Bodkin said.

"You're kidding."

"Why would I?"

"I think you're in close quarters with some bad actors up there, Lee. This Center for Defense Maneuvers is known to fly under the radar. They use alternative names sometimes, including the Natural Materials one," Lita said. "In terms of their project, they pass it off as 'wolf reintroduction,' supposedly to lend help for an endangered species. Which is a line. The areas where these initiatives are done have been crawling with wolves already. Timber wolves, the kind that belong there. It appears that the new ones eat the native wolves up."

Same thing Mickey had suggested.

"The U.S. Fish and Wildlife Service know about this?" Bodkin asked.

"Yes. But this other agency is for some reason authorized to go right over their head," Lita said. "They don't sound like they're really doing any defense maneuvers."

"Kind of like the Department of Homeland Security keeping us secure?"

"Pretty much. Especially during one of the TSA airport striptease drills."

"It's kind of hot sometimes, when a Large Marge carries it out," Bodkin said.

"For you, maybe. In any event, we don't know what the ultimate objective is of these wolfpack plantings," Lita said. "But let's go back to the federal guys keeping a low profile near you now."

"I don't have any names yet. Any I should be on the lookout for?" Bodkin said.

"Yes, an important one. The operations leader. Some guy named Wirth. Darrell Wirth. Former U.S. Army major. Received a dishonorable discharge years back. Thought sadism was part of the job description. But he's got federal government contacts, plus some seedy allies on the military side of things. Including assassins from foreign governments, some players in the Russian mob."

"The situation as a whole doesn't sound good,"

Bodkin said. "And this operations leader, Major Wirth, must be a real class act."

"Worse than it sounds. When you hear the things he himself has done, those others don't sound so bad," Lita said. "He's not in it for the integrity of the country, trust me."

"Love of country second, profit first," Bodkin offered.

"It's all for profit," Lita said. "No love of country needed. A shadow government type of deal; a splinter group, you could say. These are some bad guys, Lee. Over your head, maybe."

Bodkin didn't like what she'd just said. Maybe Lita was right, but to hell with it. Up against some military reject: over his head? He was staying. At the end of this outing, the town would be celebrating with killer wolf stir-fry. They could count on it.

"Surely you jest, my dear," Bodkin said, trying to sound at ease. "We'll get the job done despite the intruding flunkies, trust me."

"I'm serious. If it turns out it's this Wirth creep and his hired hands, maybe you should bail on it. Let state police step in or something. Maybe the FBI."

"I don't know. Not my usual way of proceeding."

"At least tell Gladdis everything I told you. Let her decide on her own. You owe her."

True. He owed Lita and Gladdis both for any semblance of a life, for the grip on sanity. Couldn't admit it to them, though.

"Will do, babe. I'll tell her."

"If they're representatives from this Center for Defense Maneuvers effort, consider quitting and coming home. You have backordered longbows anyway. Catch up."

True, again. *Damn.* He pictured the triumphant look

in that hulking charcoal grey wolf, its amber eyes burning bright, as it watched Gladdis and Sheba plunge over the cliff, and Bodkin prepare to do the same. Not like a canine; something more intelligent. Much more so. He wasn't going to let that demon outdo him.

Lita, I love you my dear, but forget about it.

"I'll think on it. Looking like a 'no' at this point, though."

A pause. "Promise to keep me warm when you get back?" Lita said.

"Write me in for it, *mi amore.*"

Bodkin ended the call, then let the phone rest in his lap. He'd stay and complete the job, then receive a payout from the small department up here; risking life and limb for an amount that was marginal at best. What was wrong with him? Gladdis would hear the details later; for now she stared into her coffee cup, half asleep. He peered out the hotel room window, past the row of sugar maple trees that lined up there in the semi-dark, to the dim view of the unending lake beyond. Staring through the gloom at woods, water, and nothing. Thinking, sorting things out, evaluating what he and Gladdis had unwittingly stepped into. Maybe plunged into.

Nine

Three blocks away, at the Maxitel Suites motel, Lee Bodkin's call had just been hijacked. Darrell Wirth scribbled a few notes on a notepad, then looked up at the other two men. Melvin Tarko looked back at him, no emotion on his face. Waiting. Victor Dudnik just looked at the ceiling, with an expression both peaceful and pleased.

Their special interceptor device, cooperating with a satellite far from the earth's surface, collected the cell phone communication and transmitted it through the device's receiver. The gadget rested on top of the room's little refrigerator; it looked like a small battery charger or some kind of diagnostic tool, nothing special. But it was in fact quite special, and perfect for Wirth's counter-surveillance tactics. Lives had been altered and even ended due to its eavesdropping abilities.

Each of the three men had attached a listening device to their ears. When the call ended, they slipped them off. The room was quiet for a few seconds.

"He knows, so he goes," Wirth said.

"Just like that?" asked Tarko.

"Yes, just like that," replied Wirth.

"I advise caution, Major Wirth. The Homeland Security folks said this guy is a pretty bad motherfucker," Dudnik said. "They've used him for work a couple of times, so they'd know."

Wirth rested his eyes on Dudnik. The thug, the Albanian peasant. Sitting here now, on the edge of lecturing a major in the U.S. Army. A former major, actually. He'd been discharged – they'd accused him of unauthorized torture in a past Venezuelan incident – but the charges were nonsense. Rules were meant to be bent, but the brass was so inflexible sometimes. But, whatever.

"I'm just saying, maybe we should work around the tough guy," Dudnik said. "By the time we've captured the animal and left, he'll just be figuring things out."

"I can handle said tough guy, as you refer to him," Wirth said.

"Can you?"

"My friend, don't mistake me for some West Point ninny. I earned my rank, I didn't attend some college ROTC program for it. I was part of the 78th Ranger Regiment. Heard of it?"

"Oh yes. You must be a certifiable killing machine, boss," Dudnik said.

"You sound a bit sarcastic, there, Sergeant Dudnik. It was sergeant, correct?"

"Sergeant, yes, for whatever difference it made. I'm not being disrespectful. I meant it. I admire you," Dudnik said. He smiled. Wirth felt a moment of discomfort, the ruthless sane man interacting with a genuine lunatic. But, the lunatic was the one exercising more caution than he himself was. Hmm. Complicated: put a determined sociopath in a small motel room with a calculating psychopath, which one would win?

"Easy does it, men," Tarko said. "With all due respect, sir," he said, looking at Wirth. Then, "On a related note, what about the blonde?

"We didn't count on her," Wirth said. "No idea who she is. Yet. But no need to worry; probably just his squeeze."

"The one on the phone actually sounded like she was," Tarko said.

"Then maybe his assistant. Maybe he has two. Way more trouble than it's worth to take her out, in any case. But if she causes trouble..."

"Then we know what to do. I look forward to it," Dudnik said, then he smiled again. Wirth could see subtle satisfaction in it. Yep, he'd picked the right guys for this job, especially this Albanian; someone comfortable with killing a noncombatant was important here. Even more so, a person who accepted what a maneating mutant wolf could do. Accept it, then proceed to defend that very wolf. It appeared the other guy, Melvin Tarko, the assassin from Moldova, was on board too. He was reputed to be the consummate professional. Not crazy, just merciless and obedient. Nice.

So the civilian hires staying over in the other motel, the guy with his sandpaper meathead and his blonde girlfriend tagging along, now knew about Operation Red Fang. With just a little more info, they would know about the special specimen, Product 68Q. That would be less than ideal. The two of them, with their light armaments and swollen overconfidence, were basically hikers with guns as far as he was concerned. The guy was supposed to be some kind of bounty hunter. Yeah, sure, if he said so. But he wasn't military, that much was certain. When Wirth heard about the guy going after the wolfpack with a mere hunter's shotgun, he'd had to smile. Such comedy; surprising that the dunce was still alive.

In any event, the two civilian morons knew too much. They'd put up little resistance in an altercation against just Wirth himself, and much less now with these two Eastern European nutcases on the job. And the two bounty hunting hobbyists had just made themselves a liability, increasing the motivation for their elimination.

Had to take care of the He-Man first, this Bodman or Bodlin or whoever. He was on record as the hero for hire; the Fed's own internal affairs vigilantes would consult with him when seeking answers. Had to prevent that. Wirth's employees here, Dudnik and Tarko, would help with those details. After that – and once the wolf specimen was apprehended, that was key – the two females would also be targeted for elimination. He'd leave his two hitmen out of it; transfer the money to their accounts, then have the project's transport vehicle come and take them to the airport. Wirth would then carry out the eliminations of the women himself. Take no chances. The blonde one up here in town first, and then whoever that chick on the phone was. They didn't have her identified yet, but Wirth had the location. Down in St. Paul, just a few hours drive. He'd see what headquarters said; after Product 68Q was collected and secured, he could shoot the two women where he found them and disappear. Nobody would have the first clue where to start looking. And if they did, the Center for Defense Maneuvers would run interference for him.

Well, the assignment as a whole was taking shape, and to Wirth it didn't seem that bad. He had the green light for some abductions and some killing, both Darrell Wirth favorites. Plus the monitoring of a field experiment, in which a few rural people who didn't matter ended up dead. That last part was neither good nor bad, all just part of the specimen testing. The testing was wonderful, of course, as it involved a really nifty, ornery beast created from a government endeavor. A beast he'd soon show who was boss as he waylaid it and brought it in from the field. Best of all, the operations people at headquarters didn't care who got hurt, as long as the mission was achieved. Wirth was in his element.

Ten

Bodkin wandered to the window from the hotel bed, the ancient wooden floor creaking with each step. The sun was just coming up over the lake, a dazzling orange-pink orb, its brilliance not yet shining off the snow along the shore. An hour from now it would be. By then, he and Gladdis would be back up in the hills, going for round two against the pack. This time more strategically; hopefully no contact with the beasts at all. Save a showdown for when their backup weapons arrived. The lever-action rifles they'd been lent were excellent for so many things, but they simply didn't have the capacity needed at the present time, holding just five bullets in their magazine. For normal conditions – and targets – that would be fine, but it was obvious he and Gladdis were up against an exceptional situation here. They'd play it in a more conservative manner for now.

Today would be mainly a scouting trip. Bodkin believed he could set the maneating canine attackers up for a fall, in a big way, but he had to verify some things. That would require going back out, getting close once again to the belly of the beast. Hopefully they wouldn't end up inside of it.

He touched his hand to Sheba's snout. The dog had also just arisen, but looked more chipper than Bodkin felt. Even after her chilly swim yesterday, Sheba looked ready to go...as a matter of fact, she didn't look bothered in the least. That was pretty much the usual: upstaging him. Of course, the alternative would be worse. Would he want a dog that was useless but easy on his ego, or an ornery wolf-dog he could barely keep up with? The fact that he was still alive was the best answer. A kindly, polite dog wouldn't last long in their current business.

Bodkin felt a bit beaten up, but he was ready for action as well. Sore, yeah, but again nothing new here. Too many years of these unpredictable assignments where things go haywire; you had to go forward or drop out of this lifestyle. If you stayed in the lifestyle – this routine of simple bounty hunting assignments suddenly turning into a sort of special ops melee – and didn't rise to the occasion, you'd probably die. Get with it or get the hell out. Despite last night's ambushed-by-fangs shock and the resulting comedy of errors, Bodkin was in fact in the process of getting with it. Getting his stuff ready, his mind coming back into the zone. One key ingredient was not yet here in the room with him though.

Just a burst of caffeine in his bloodstream and he'd be good. Maybe a straight triple espresso, a drink as common to Bodkin as a can of soda pop was to many others. Bring back one of the same to Gladdis's room, and both of their engines would be purring and ready for action in no time.

A little drive-through kiosk sat in a convenience store parking lot just two doors down. They called themselves Thundercloud Coffee, Bodkin believed; the name itself suggested intense caffeine. Yum. Bodkin figured it would be open before the sun came up, typical of coffee vendors, and decided to walk to it.

Sheba stepped along with him to the door, but Bodkin stroked her face twice, then pushed her away. The dog knew what it meant: stay. He'd be walking up to a drive-through to order; awkward enough without a dog, with cars and trucks pulling in to do the same.

"I'll be right back, girl." He'd put on jeans, his hiking boots, and a medium weight Carhartt jacket over his t-shirt. It wasn't an outfit warm enough for the weather, not even close to the bundling they'd be wrapped in later for the outing. But this scamper for espresso would be quick. Just a couple of minutes.

Man plans, and God laughs.

The abduction was quick, and in Bodkin's opinion, pretty well orchestrated. He thought it completely sucked at the same time, mainly because he wasn't the one doing the takedown.

A hunched-over fisherman, slender and a little taller than Bodkin, walked with head down, wearing a heap of old garments. The kind of clothes that worked in inclement weather but that a person didn't mind getting fish odors on. Sporting a long-brimmed ball cap, pulled down to partly occlude his face, in Bodkin's experience typical of antisocial, loner fishermen. His free arm swung in a lazy manner, the other clutched two long fishing rods. He looked tired, distracted, maybe hung over. Walked on a path that would intercept Bodkin, and seemed somehow to increase his stride as they approached each other in the open parking lot. As the two neared each other, the hunched over guy with the fishing poles slowed and raised his head just enough to make momentary eye contact. He looked annoyed, and waved a hand, both impatient and dismissive, indicating Bodkin should go ahead. And get out of his way, finally.

The garments, the fatigued posture, and the look of annoyance on the other man all sold Bodkin on the fakeout. He nodded and stepped past the fisherman, the impatient curmudgeon. He was down on the cold surface of the parking lot in a state of electrified paralysis four seconds later.

Melvin Tarko was relieved. The bulky figure of Lee Bodkin collapsed, still fully awake but neutralized by the Taser stun gun. Temporarily, of course. Had to hurry. As Wirth gunned the minivan from the far side of the lot, Tarko prepared to heave Bodkin's bulk up and through the side door of the vehicle. Tarko knew overtaking this man had not been guaranteed. Unlike Wirth, Tarko trusted the reports from their government contacts about this ruffian. They'd said, pretty clearly, that if it came down to hand-to-hand with Bodkin, the best chance of surviving was to run. Fast and far. He was pretty good with weapons as well, but in general, in a barehanded scuffle against him, the great majority of men had no chance. Not a slight chance or steep odds; they'd said it would be hopeless.

Tarko therefore didn't like being the one to walk close by and issue the zap to Bodkin, but in his three-person team, what choice was there? The arrogant Major Wirth would probably walk up and stand face-to-face with the target, then poke his finger in the guy's chest in a challenge before attempting the stun gun shot. What a joke. And then there was that lunatic Dudnik, who did in fact take Bodkin seriously. But he was clearly nuts, and he loved killing people too much, based on the way he told his stories of conflicts in the former Yugoslavia. If he was the one to do the stun gun assault, Dudnik might take his knife to the target once it was subdued. Didn't want Bodkin dead, not yet anyway. Between Dudnik and Wirth, one with delusions of grandeur and the other preoccupied with a bloodlust urge, Tarko wasn't sure which man was a greater threat to their success.

Oh, well. His own play-acting had worked. He'd stolen a couple of fishing rigs from a boat nearby, then pretended he was an alcoholic outcast, a hardcore loser who fished on the pier all day. People rarely noticed guys like that, and when they did, usually wrote them off. Seemed even the incomparable Bodkin character had. He may not have blown operations much in the past, but Bodkin had messed up this time...in the presence of Melvin Tarko, no less. Many before him had done the same, and there'd been no second chance for any of them. Others he'd been assigned to kill, but this one was to be taken alive. In this case, accordingly, he'd nailed the target right in the back of the neck with the Taser. Excellent.

The team's van, with its smoked windows and plain white finish, slammed to a stop next to where Tarko stood. Out of the van's side door jumped Dudnik, handcuffs already out. By the time he crouched next to Bodkin, Tarko had flipped Bodkin onto his front and pulled his immobile arms back behind him. Dudnik clicked the cuffs on, and the two hired thugs lifted Bodkin with some effort and shoved him into the waiting van. The side door slammed shut, the vehicle lunged from the parking lot, and the area was taken over once again by silence and ice-cold breeze. Only two fishing rods, recently stolen and now cast aside, showed any sign that an event had just transpired here at all.

Eleven

The four men trudged through the dense forest, each step whisking fluffy snow up off its frozen floor. As the effects of the Taser wore off, Bodkin felt like throwing up, but he didn't want to waste the energy doing so. He purposely gave off the signs of defeat, of being downtrodden and whipped. He made a sad and discouraged look, head drooping. But it was an act. He was on edge, still a bit in disbelief of how easy he'd been grabbed. But he wasn't conceding here, not in the slightest. On the contrary, Bodkin was looking for the opportunity to kill his captors and escape. Or just escape. Then kill them later.

Wirth and Tarko carried folding tranquilizer guns, which they'd stored in their rucksacks until they'd made it out into the concealment of the woods. On each man's hip rested a holster sheathing a semi-automatic pistol. Dudnik hoisted no tranquilizer, only a pistol, now out of its holster; it had been adorned with a black sound suppressor on its end. Typical gangster equipment. Wirth hiked in front of Bodkin, and the other two stayed behind him.

"Dudnik, keep back from Tarko several steps. If this blockhead here runs or kicks at us or anything, finish him. No matter where we are on the trail, and whether or not he's showed us the region of the wolf lair. Empty that pistol into him, then reload; hit him again if needed," Darrell Wirth said.

He just stated their names in front of me...proving my long-term survival odds aren't looking good, thought Bodkin.

"Got that, bounty hunter boy?" Wirth said to Bodkin.

"Loud and clear. I've been here with you the whole time, after all," Bodkin replied.

"Cheeky. You're real clever with your comebacks. Not for long," Wirth said.

"So you marching me out for secretive disposal or what? Why walk way out in the woods for it?" Bodkin said.

"You're just needed to steer us to the center of the activity. To the special wolfpack." Wirth then smiled. "Team effort. To make this lakeside community safer."

"Why are you here if you have no idea how to proceed? What help can I be?"

"Sir, how much in the dark do you believe we are? We know you interfaced with the pack yesterday," Wirth said. "Amazing you're still here. Anyway, we need to know the area from which they approached. We haven't the luxury to spend a week here determining such information. So your help is requested. We knew assertive action would be needed to get that help from you."

"So why the silenced heater?" Bodkin said, looking at the thick 10 mm pistol in Dudnik's hand, the 4-inch silencer stuck onto its muzzle.

"It's just in case you get obstreperous," Dudnik replied, lighting up with a smile.

Charming. Wonder if your smile will last. Bodkin pictured several of Dudnik's gleaming teeth smashed out of his mouth. The momentary image brought Bodkin a tiny bit of elation, especially since in the daydream those teeth had just been kicked out of the enemy's head with Bodkin's steel-toed boot. Nice. It's the little things that help you get through tough times.

"Oh, and Bodsen or Bokken or whatever your name is," Wirth said. "Try anything, and I'll make an 'X' across your face with this." He brandished a military-issue knife,

a flat black finish muting any shine along its 7-inch blade.
"You dig?"

"Yeah, I dig, groovy guy," Bodkin said. He looked
into Wirth's eyes with a calm intensity that made Wirth
happy about the cuffs on the captive's wrists.

"Yeah, uh, just so we have that straight," Wirth said.

***

"Took quite a bit of trial and error, but in the
breeding process the researchers finally made a
breakthrough," Wirth said.

"So it's kind of a Franken-wolf, then," Bodkin said.

"More like a super wolf. All natural ingredients. Pure
genetic engineering, with some notable contributors.
You wouldn't believe the combination of dog creatures,
and some other things, if I told you," Wirth said. "Know
anything about genetics?"

"Some. Had one class in college, during the two
semesters I was enrolled. I liked it," Bodkin said.

"Were you planning to be some kind of science
genius or something?" asked Wirth.

"No, I basically majored in wrestling," Bodkin said.

"Figures," Wirth said.

The men had begun a descent now, veering down a
snowy hillside through the brush, small saplings, and
towering maple trees, approaching the bottoms of the
Maelstrom River. Bodkin was feeling the chill, a little on
his trunk, but much more so on his uncovered ears and
hands. Couldn't worry about it now, though. Every
second counted. Looking for an opening, an idea, to gain
his freedom. Then kill these pieces of garbage.

"The project is called Operation Red Fang," Wirth
said. "I'd like to say it'll bring our fine country glory, but
really, it's just for the money."

They plodded along, Wirth still in the lead, Tarko still immediately behind Bodkin, watching closely. Dudnik continued to stay back a few paces, as a safety net to shoot Bodkin if he escaped. The hiking was grueling, but to Dudnik, the rest of this seemed fun. He couldn't wait for Bodkin's finale, which he was personally assigned to.

"So you folks refer to your mad scientist spawn as 'Red Fang'? Or is it only the project's name?" Bodkin asked.

"Both. This current specimen is the only one worthy of bearing the name," Wirth said. "But officially, he's been titled Product 68Q."

"That official name certainly embraces the spirit of nature," Bodkin said.

Wirth looked back in disapproval, Tarko appraised Bodkin without emotion, and Dudnik smiled. Again.

***

"Drones, bombs, missiles, they all have their place," said Wirth. "But so often, in any war, the action comes down to infantry. Yes, even in modern day, infantry." Wirth glanced back at Bodkin, the start of a twisted smile on his face.

"The mighty wolf infantry, huh?" Bodkin said.

"Most certainly. Imagine a pack 300, 400 strong, led by a supreme leader. If they all get taken out, you just replace them. Wolves strike fear in the heart of humankind more so than any other person could do. Especially if they eat people. One way or another, we'll get it perfected," Wirth said.

"The big dreams of the honorable Mr. Wirth. Or, I guess that should be dishonorable," Bodkin said.

Wirth spun and held the fighting knife's point in front of Bodkin's nose. "Just keep it up, you rent-a-soldier punk. I'll start the carving now," Wirth said.

"Thought you needed my insight," Bodkin said.

"We can use it, but we don't need it. Plus, you'll still help, like it or not, even if a couple of slices adorn your homely mug," Wirth said.

"That hurts, Mr. Wirth. Homely?" Bodkin said. He turned to Tarko. "What do you think, sir? Do I look that drab?" Tarko maintained a straight face and nudged Bodkin forward, extending his arm but keeping the rest of his body back to do it. In order to maintain distance and draw his weapon, just in case. Behind Tarko, Dudnik chuckled.

"Anyway, Major Wirth, you were saying?" Bodkin said.

"That I'll slice you up?"

"No, regarding your grand experiment. You're here in town, to what, soothe your laboratory wolf monster? What's the story?"

"You're pretty curious aren't you? Well, explaining things to you won't matter in the long run," Wirth said.

Knew it. They plan to ice me out here. Of course, that's the only option that would make sense, Bodkin thought. For him to now pass up an opening for an escape attempt would be foolish, handcuffs or not, life-threatening or not. No other hope than to try. But, how? Almost any fleeing action would be suicide. Bodkin pictured the violent flowage of the Maelstrom River, with him being carried away by the river to safety. But the details had yet to be filled in.

"So basically," continued Wirth. "Your run-in was with the wolfpack led by Product 68Q. He's big and mean. And smart. As I said earlier, he's looking like our best result ever. We need him."

"Smart, huh? Can it tell if a soldier's gun is loaded or empty?"

"Of course. That's one of the first things we've taught any of the alpha specimens. When empty, the actions stay open on automatics, and even on other guns, the owner of it starts to act differently when the gun runs dry. Among other things, the shooter always – always – looks at the action of the firearm."

As Bodkin had done. So that was how it knew, during that first attack. "This one wolf in particular is so crucial? I'm picturing a whole kennel full of similar canines somewhere," Bodkin said.

"No, not anymore. When put in with similar wolves to socialize, he killed them. All of them."

"I'd hate to see the bill for his chew toys," Bodkin said.

"He's a determined animal. Our ultimate alpha wolf so far. We bring him in successfully, and we're set," Wirth said.

"And the sale to some foreign government will then commence," Bodkin said.

"Precisely. To the highest bidder."

"Even to enemy countries?" Bodkin said.

"We don't care. Cash talks, not ideals. So yes, the product will be up for sale. Very perceptive, for a low-life such as yourself. How'd you know?"

"You said it was for profit. I couldn't picture sales being made only to pet shops. Foreign militaries would be logical."

"Yes. And you'll have been part of the testing. Picture yourself as a contributor to your government. Feel proud," Wirth said.

"I picture when this is all over I'll be roasting a big freak of a wolf on a spit, dishing out sections of its tenderloin on paper plates to the town folk. Taconite Bluff's first wolf roast," Bodkin said.

"Nothing wrong with thinking big," Wirth said. "But

you're a bit delusional."

We'll see.

"So no hair on your precious little wolf's head can be touched. Correct? Need to bring him in unharmed, give him a pat on the head and a doggy biscuit, maybe," Bodkin said.

"How limited do you think our effort is here, dummy? We'd like 68Q alive, for further behavioral exercises, but we don't absolutely need that. It's his DNA that is crucial," Wirth said. "The current sample we had mutated for some reason, so we need Red Fang's DNA as it exists now. With it we can replicate over and over. Without it, well, we have to start all over again. Plus, we need the big wolf's body, to keep it out of the hands of any competitors."

"I would think the rest of the pack would share a similar DNA, being from the same looney bin kennel system," Bodkin said.

"The rest of the wolfpack isn't from our lab. They're simply Arctic wolves, from the northernmost reaches of Russia. Captured as pups."

"And now very big hombres," Bodkin said.

"Oh yeah. Nothing like these medium-sized wolves native to America. The critters we introduced in this locale can easily overcome an American timber wolf."

"What if they wipe out a native population?" Bodkin said. "These ecosystems took thousands of years to establish."

"Tough," Wirth said. "In Idaho and up in Ontario, our group has done similar projects. Those areas lost some elk and moose. I heard some people vanished too. I couldn't care less. As a matter of fact, we knew Minnesota had a healthy wolf population. One of the reasons it was chosen for Operation Red Fang."

"Because it already had wolves? I don't follow,"

Bodkin said.

"To see how well our new wolfpack, especially Product 68Q, could annihilate an existing group of wolves," Wirth said. "They've not had much problem so far."

Bodkin, despite his fatigue and attention to survival, wanted to respond with a put-down. But he simply couldn't think of anything, once confronted with the extent of the evil these guys had planned. Wipe out an entire ecosystem...for a fistful of cash?

"But as you alluded to, Bodsen, Product 68Q is crucial. We need to neutralize him during today's effort. Once we have him tranquilized, we assume the pack will then have no leadership. They'll simply retreat."

"Have you interacted with this pack before?" asked Bodkin, remembering the wolves' organized ferocity. Incredulous toward Wirth's clueless approach. But he didn't say so; he really wanted to see Wirth get mangled.

"No. But no problem anticipated, my friend. I was Special Forces once, you realize. These vermin have never been other than a handful of savage beasts used by our group. Manipulated; we did it before, we'll do it today," Wirth said. "And if Product 68Q is too much trouble, we simply kill him. Not optimal, but easier. It's that DNA we need, not the living beast."

Less than a half-hour later, they came upon the bluff where he, Montrose, and Sheba were first attacked. Bodkin now viewed it from below, but the rise stood out, easily the highest bluff along this section of the Maelstrom River. The rest of the hills and ridges were equally full of life, loaded with pine, maple, and oak, but cowered below the big bluff in terms of height. No mistaking it.

"There ya go, boys. The bluff where all the action took place," Bodkin said.

"Where'd they come from? What direction did they intercept you and the blonde when they attacked?" Wirth said.

"Not this low. There are at least a couple of benches, small plateaus, up the hill from right here. They used one of those as their main thoroughfare to get close to us. It's narrow, with a steep drop off to the side. Going through it, they pretty much had to travel single file. After that, they spread out."

"So waiting uphill from that bottleneck point would give a shooter their choice of wolves to aim at?"

"In theory, yes. But with these critters, who knows. Pretty amazing how organized they carried out the onslaught."

"Product 68Q was well-trained even as a puppy to organize other canines. Not amazing at all, when you know how much proven conditioning was used in the whole endeavor," Wirth said. He turned to Dudnik, established eye contact, and then nodded in the direction of the river. Dudnik stepped up and seized Bodkin high on one arm, then steered him away from the other two men. Wirth and Tarko turned and started a climb up and crossways across the slope. Looking for a wolf trail, one that would lead them to Product 68Q. To the specimen nicknamed Red Fang.

***

"Wirth and his dipshit American boys call it Product 68Q. 'Product.' Wow," Dudnik said. "Oops, sorry. You're American too, I guess. No offense intended."

"None taken," Bodkin said. *Just give me a chance to kill you and escape, and we'll be square.*

"You do seem a little, well, harder than the typical American or something. My compliments," Dudnik said.

"Coming from you that means something, Dudnik. I'm touched."

"Sure, no problem. When I was in the army, back in Albania, we noticed how the Brits were so subdued and the Yanks were so cocky. And so serious. Makes it easier that you like to joke around," Dudnik said.

"See? I'm a good guy. You can release me now."

Dudnik solidified his grip on Bodkin's arm then turned him so they were both facing straight downhill. "To the river," Dudnik said.

"Thought I was simply being brought along to point the way to the pack," Bodkin said. Although he knew better; he currently acted naive, but figured from the start they would ultimately try to snuff him. It had been suggested earlier as they progressed on the trek, and now here it was. Verified. Bodkin would soon be dead, if the trio's plans went through. Had to buy whatever seconds he could here. Keep the other guy talking.

"You're now done. Thank you. A true heartfelt thank you. Now to the river."

"You're breaking your word," Bodkin said.

"Come now, sir. You've been in this business a long time. You pretty much know how these things work," Dudnik said.

And he was right, Bodkin did. But Bodkin just replied, "Why the river?" As Bodkin said it he froze in place, refusing to step further.

"Walk," Dudnik said, grabbing Bodkin's arm a little tighter and shoving him forward. "You may be more of a bull than me, but I've got the gun and you've got the cuffs. Unfortunately for you, you're wearing them."

"Going to the river. I think I know why," Bodkin said, stopping again.

"And you'd be right," Dudnik said, touching the end of the silencer to the back of Bodkin's head. "Now move it. Everyone's gotta go some time."

"It's just...the water. I've always been afraid. Can't swim, don't want to go near it."

Bodkin actually felt fear, anxiety, and a chill of terror whispering to him. He kept it contained, but it was there. To tell the full truth, though: water was the least of his worries. The primary concern were the bullets in Dudnik's gun. And the damn handcuffs.

"Just do me here. Don't bring me any closer. I won't resist, if you just end it here. I can't be drowned. No way," Bodkin said, digging his boots into the snow. He figured – he knew, actually – Dudnik would keep pushing him. They wanted Bodkin's body to disappear, and it was far too cold to dig a grave. The river would be so convenient, especially with a small boulder dropped on top of Bodkin's dead body to pin him at the river's bottom.

"Drowning is not in the plan. I promise," Dudnik said. "You grew up here I thought. Don't you hayseeds have like 9,000 lakes in this region or something? And you're afraid of water? You're pathetic. Now move your ass." With that, Dudnik pushed up against Bodkin and thrust him forward.

Bodkin couldn't believe it. Dudnik's face actually came up next to his own when nudging him along. Perfect. This guy was supposed to be a commando? Looked like Albania's military needed some fine-tuning.

"Look, you're not strong enough to push me to the river," Bodkin said, then stopped again. They were now about 30 yards from the river's gurgling edge. "Let's talk this out. We can deal perhaps, just the two of us."

As predicted – it was inevitable really – Dudnik began another shove, this time meaning to show his strength. Like most close-combat amateurs, he believed tough gestures and machismo meant something. He

began the shove by leaning his chest hard against
Bodkin's shoulder, to give his next push some real force.
His face came up close to Bodkin's, just for an instant.

Bodkin's forehead popped back after slamming into
the bridge of Dudnik's nose, wrenching the cartilage in
the center of the target's face. Dudnik held onto his gun,
but was unconscious on his feet for a full two seconds.
One half-second before he could recover, Bodkin
dropped onto his side and into Dudnik's near leg, his
own legs wide apart and straight, the upper leg in front
of Dudnik's legs, the lower one behind. In an instant he
cut out Dudnik's footing and slammed him down. By
executing the flying leg scissors – a classic judo attack –
Bodkin had flipped Dudnik's legs skyward and his head
straight down to the rocky ground. Dudnik's head hit,
but with bleary eyes he still managed to raise the pistol
and point. As he did it, the toe section of Bodkin's boot
slammed into the gun hand, twirling the pistol away and
snapping two of Dudnik's fingers. The whole skirmish to
this point took three seconds.

Time to finish this deal. Bodkin, with cuffs still
securing his hands behind him, scrambled his body close
to Dudnik, who was still on his back but starting to rise.
Bodkin ensconced Dudnik's head and one arm with both
legs, twisting the legs tight and locking them around each
other at the ankles. Like a hangman's noose under the
weight of its falling victim, Bodkin wrenched on a leg
strangle, cranking it down with force so great his own
legs shook with the effort. Dudnik fought for a moment,
then tried to get turned in order to get up, then collapsed
as oxygenated blood was cut off from his brain.

Bodkin anticipated bullets from the other two men,
could almost feel the slugs bursting into the nearby
brush and maybe into him. No bullets yet, but he could
hear branches and leaves cracking and rustling up the

hill. The other two had sprung into action. He had a few seconds at best. He held the strangle for another instant after Dudnik passed out, then released it. To kill Dudnik would have taken another full minute of scissoring, maybe a little longer. No time now.

He backed into Dudnik's body, so his hands locked behind him could plunge into the other man's pants pocket. Nothing there, other than a stick of gum or something, plus some coins. Bodkin rolled over the awakening assailant, who had started to groan softly. Other pocket. Pushing his ice cold fingertips into the trousers was painful with the little feeling left in them...but soon he detected the little metal trinket there. The key to the handcuffs.

Bodkin plucked it out of the pocket, careful to not drop it into the snowy forest floor. He managed to hold on; after arranging the tiny stem in one hand, he snaked the tiny key into the first hole. It had to work or Bodkin was dead.

The first handcuff clicked open. He brought his arms in front, plunging the key in the other cuff as he arranged his body behind a fat tree trunk nearby. Still waiting for bullets. The other cuff was off in a moment, and he set it quietly next to him. He spied Dudnik's handgun then, five feet from the vanquished thug on the ground.

Regardless of the risk of leaving cover, Bodkin rolled to the handgun and scooped it up. Then he twirled in a crouch behind a fallen tree next to Dudnik, using the tree's mass of roots for protection.

Bodkin could still hear leaves crunching and branches breaking as the two men up the hill from him scrambled. He still assumed they were situating themselves to deliver killing shots his way, to anchor their now-uncooperative hostage. Peering through an opening in the dirt-covered tree roots, Bodkin took in the unfolding scenario. To his surprise, Wirth and Tarko weren't looking at the exchange between Dudnik and him at all. They were looking elsewhere, their attention transfixed on the steep hillside above them.

Well, well. Guess who's come for breakfast. Along the ridge, four furry heads appeared from the density, their bodies slinking from the brush and claiming the open forest floor like parasites clamoring onto a helpless host. Then another three heads materialized, followed by thick-muscled bodies, the wolves' long tails standing straight from their forms in a telltale sign of aggression. Another wolf trotted uphill from the rock structures along the river, having set itself up there to block any exit in that direction. Safe to say, Wirth and Tarko had now completely forgotten about Bodkin.

Dudnik's pistol was now in Bodkin's hand and the cuffs were off. What could Bodkin say? *Thank you for waiting, maneating wolves. Seriously.*

The wolves didn't plan to wait long. Two of the canines circled to Wirth's left, two to the right, while another came straight at him. He'd situated himself behind a thick tree trunk, flinging the rucksack with the tranquilizer gun to the ground. He now had his handgun out, ready to kill. He'd even shoot the dark grey alpha wolf, Product 68Q, if it rushed him. So much for it being his treasured creature.

Bodkin would make this a little easier for the wolfpack, just this once. The other men had quickly forgotten about him; that worked for Bodkin. For Tarko, who 13 yards uphill had positioned himself behind a tree trunk like Wirth had, not so much.

Using soft earth and the avoidance of twigs to step quietly, Bodkin left the cover of the tree roots and edged over to where Dudnik lay, still senseless from Bodkin's strangling move. He made sure he had a clear opening through the brush and branches to where Tarko cowered behind the big tree, then pointed the handgun down at Dudnik's face and shot him once between the eyes. Next Bodkin raised the pistol, not able to aim exactly with the fat silencer blocking out the pistol's sights, but still able to estimate. It would do the trick.

Upon his shot into Dudnik, the pistol had made a subdued cough instead of emitting a blast, but it was enough to make Tarko glance back, probably to yell an order at Dudnik as the wolves closed in. His eyes instead met Bodkin's, just as the first bullet was launched his way. It hit Tarko in the cheekbone, whipping his head against the tree with a thud. Bodkin fired at him again, hitting him twice in the chest. Tarko's body collapsed just as the first wolf arrived, the beast unaware its intended victim was now a warm, lifeless body. It covered Tarko and tore into his neck, before turning its attention to Bodkin, who kept the wolf in sight as he estimated the arrival of the others.

They were preoccupied with Wirth, closing on him from three sides. In the instant Bodkin could appraise the scene, it looked like Wirth had only dropped one. With eight or nine attackers now trying to sink their fangs into him, putting only one animal down simply wasn't going to help. Wirth was quickly covered and conquered by the wolves.

Sorry wolf, he thought to the one nearest to him. Your companions have abandoned you, as interested as they are in eating the major. Bodkin planted two slugs in the base of its neck, the powerful but muffled shots making his hand jerk as he squeezed the trigger. The wolf collapsed forward in a heap, twitching.

As Bodkin scrambled to the sharp rock formations lining the river, the pack stopped attacking the other men. Bodkin heard the half-howl sound emit from the charcoal alpha wolf, one which signaled a serious attack was about to commence. In this case, with all available sets of fangs interested in the only man here still alive. The alpha wolf, aka Product 68Q, glared at Bodkin, staying halfway behind a patch of brush, while the other wolves surged into the open. To the edge of the river, to their waiting prey. He raised the pistol and popped off the remaining bullets – it turned out to be six – and killed two more of the predators. Then the bristling pack reached the rocks and lunged up to seize him.

He glanced for a half-second at the surface of the ice cold, rust-stained Maelstrom River, swirling and swelling like a flowing torrent of chilled, frothy root beer.

Frigid river, I hate you and love you at the same time, thought Bodkin, diving into the water, letting its unstoppable force sweep him away. Down toward the giant lake and to safety. Away from his attackers, both living and dead, canine and human.

***

"Don't let this become a pattern, Bodkin. Why don't you just walk down to your hotel?" Mickey Manoomin said.

"It's five blocks away. I might be frozen solid by then," Bodkin said, soggy and trembling as the hypothermia started its process. Second day in a row.

"You say that like it's a bad thing. Get your thick skull in here," Mickey said, stepping back and opening the door to his house's hallway. His face held a look of disdain, but he nonetheless opened a nearby closet and withdrew a wool blanket from a hanger. Itchy and dry, a perfect covering to use for a man who was wet and cold and in the first stages of freezing to death. He stepped to Bodkin, who had plopped in exhaustion on the bench there, and slung the blanket over his shoulders.

"Take it you saw some action," Mickey said.

"Quite a bit during this last session," Bodkin said, starting to visibly shiver. The blanket had arrived just in time.

"Wolves or people?"

"Both."

"I think I know which people."

"You'd be correct," Bodkin said.

"Still have a people problem?"

"Regarding said threesome who came into town, no."

"You're a mess Bodkin, but in some ways, definitely effective," Mickey said.

"I have my moments. Some four-legged adversaries still afoot, mind you."

"Wish I could help. But..." Mickey said, a rare look of apology coming over his face.

"Don't worry; I got it under control," Bodkin said, shivering some more.

"Yeah, I can tell," Mickey said.

"If you need the full details, I stopped here first for an additional reason. I actually have to scout things out over at the hotel from a distance. I assume Gladdis is OK, but I really don't know. Use your phone?"

Twelve

"Turns out they intercepted a couple of our calls...my hunch is conversation between me and you, then between me and Lita," Bodkin said.

"See? Like I've said before, you talk too much," Gladdis Montrose said.

"Uh, yeah. Ha ha. I believe they never determined who Lita was; never had you fully identified either. But you were accessible to them, being here now and all, and I couldn't picture them having had good intentions."

"'Having had'?" Montrose said. "You mean having?"

"Past tense."

"Careful there, bud. Who says they're not doing some eavesdropping right now?"

"One, this is a landline. Two, I don't think they'll be doing any intercepting any time soon."

"Thus you refer to them in past tense. Is that like in never again?" Montrose said.

"I would assume that's the case. Unless they can perform surveillance from inside the belly of a wolf."

"Whoa. You have been busy. The beasts got involved?"

"Inadvertently, they helped out," Bodkin said. "Then I took another swim."

"You really like that river, don't you? A great story to hear, I'm sure."

"And it is, in fact. Things can get a little strange sometimes."

"Yep, and the Bodkin factor increases the likelihood of strange. You at your favorite cafe?" Montrose said.

"I am. Exiled to the back room, but no charge for the phone usage," Bodkin said.

"You two used to avoid each other," Montrose said.

"We did. But now I just can't stay away," Bodkin said.

"So any developments during your unplanned outing?"

"I reaffirmed where the pack exits and enters their primary sheltering area. How they come and go from their lair deep in the brush. The findings will come in handy tomorrow," Bodkin said.

"What do we do tomorrow?"

"Tell you over lunch. Today sounds like a great day to sample that steelhead fillet special they have posted in the window at the Big Wave Broiler. They often coat their fish in a chive and black pepper batter, I've heard. After we eat, we're off to the Tugboat Fish Cannery," Bodkin said.

"Uh, Lee my man, didn't you almost die just awhile ago?" Montrose said.

"Yep, and I need rejuvenation. Need my strength back. Need to warm up. Plus, I need that paycheck," Bodkin said.

"There's the spirit. You've got me curious, in any case. Sounds like you've been processing your new findings," Montrose said.

"Very much so. And I have a plan."

***

"We need a supply of something that will aid in our cause," Bodkin said to Gladdis Montrose. He was now in dry clothes – back to his original outfit.

The breeze flowed steadily off the massive lake and ensconced them on the waterfront boardwalk; Lake Superior's whitecaps were now at their highest and most pronounced since they'd arrived, each crash of the waves into the shore's boulders sounding like a car wreck.

"And that would be...?" Montrose replied.

"Fish remains. I'm thinking fish heads in particular, for ease of use." Bodkin looked down the shore, past a row of shops to a small factory. Then to a medium sized front office structure attached to a larger pole building, where the actual processing work was done. The Tugboat Fish Cannery.

"Not sure I can talk them out of a portion though. Probably against some regulation or another. Those guys working there look like some hardcore blokes, too. Plus, I don't know a soul in the cannery industry up here," Bodkin said.

"If they actually knew you, your chances would probably decrease," Montrose said.

"That's likely."

"How much we need?"

"Just a box-full; even a small box would do."

"I'll take care of it," Montrose said.

"How ya gonna do that?" Bodkin asked.

"Venture a guess," Montrose said, then looked straight at Bodkin. Her countenance transformed before him. The intense face relaxed, the windburn on it from the elements looking all of a sudden like carefully applied color. With her blonde hair dancing in the wind, the expression suddenly looked...fetching. Blue eyes catching the sunlight, adjusting for the brightness they then looked like...bedroom eyes, you could say, if a person's mind went there. Bodkin's did for one-third of a second, felt a little flutter of something inside, then he squelched it. He had seen her strike that pose before. But under the current circumstances – unrelenting cold, scheming feds, unannounced swims in a chilly river, maneaters in the hills of above them – the transformation was pretty remarkable. Like Bodkin, Gladdis Montrose had learned long ago to do what was necessary.

"You're not supposed to do that to me, remember?" Bodkin said.

"Like the plan or what?" Montrose said. Her gaze didn't change.

"Well, I'm definitely awake now," Bodkin said.

"That's the idea."

"You'll be acquiring resources by purposely misleading other people."

"Huh. This from the guy who thinks lying like a rug is a strategy."

"Pragmatic tactics."

"Well, consider what I'm trying to get from them," Montrose said.

"A box of fish heads. Yeah, I guess the boys won't be too crushed," Bodkin said. "Cool. Head over there. But first..."

"What?"

"Give me a spin," Bodkin said, looking over her shape with mock appreciation. Well, not completely mock.

"You know what part of you I'll give a spin," Montrose said, raising one steel-toed boot off the ground, pointing to his groin.

"Don't I," Bodkin said. "All right. Get out of here."

"And you go call in that order," Montrose said, stepping away. A little killer going into her sexy act.

"Consider it done," Bodkin said.

Thirteen

They claimed their organization was just a restaurant business. Any seemingly untoward activities which might occur – allegedly – in tying up loose ends were all just part of doing business. The Cardinali family had maintained this claim for well over 100 years at this point. It had started around the year 1900 as a takeout restaurant in downtown St. Paul, Minnesota to serve Irish and Italian dock workers. It later blossomed into one of the city's most popular eating establishments.

With business slowing around the time of the Great Depression, it wasn't long until the Cardinalis branched out into, well, other profitable areas. In their minds, it was just survival, just business. Dealings, negotiations, and proposals never went smoothly every time for any company or organization, regardless of the industry. Why should their restaurant, and its related operations, be any different? At times, pressure, stubbornness, secrecy, and belligerence were called for against the competition. In special situations, lawsuits were in order. And in extreme situations, the other party might be made an offer they couldn't refuse. The free market was a rough thing. Always had been, always would be.

The term "mafia" was never uttered with any serious intent around Cardinali's Cucina, unless some work of cinema was being discussed. The members of their organization would consider playing *The Godfather* an act of silliness. Kids' stuff. But all in all, were their tactics much different than those in gangster films? Who knew? So much of it was a matter of opinion, with final decisions being made by the court system. Using that as a measuring stick, neither of the owners, the Cardinali brothers Geno and Maximo, had ever done prison time. None. But that was another story.

If members of the business community and local residents disapproved of their business protocol or their restaurant, they could simply stay away. But few people did.

Staying away is what Bodkin knew he should do, but for years, he never did. Ate there, hung out there, socialized there. He maintained proximity, knowing he might fall into temptation again. And sure enough, a situation would come up where they needed him, along with his unusual skill sets. With the right incentives, Bodkin often complied, stacking the deal always in his own favor. By a large margin.

Under no circumstances would he do a hit for them. Limits had to be set. Bodkin had a hard time doing that with food but an easy time doing it with murder. And Bodkin never accepted cash, ever. That would be illegal in most cases, plus taking it utilized no foresight. Instead, he played it for the long haul. No cash. Bodkin instead accumulated favors. Much, much more valuable. Like in the situation he and Montrose now faced.

He had two favors stored up with the Cardinali brothers, and he was calling them both in now. He phoned in to the switchboard – a backroom of the restaurant – then waited for a callback on a special line from someone with pull.

It was Maximo. Second in charge, first in lethality.

"So we owe you a couple of favors? I don't follow," Maximo said.

"The Team Dream Supreme," Bodkin said.

"What are you talking about?" Maximo said.

"It's the name of a yacht. Or, it used to be, at least."

"Oh, the hunk of junk over on the St. Croix River," Maximo said.

"Yes, Maximo. One formerly owned by some naughty St. Louis guys who sold a forbidden powder around the Midwest. Classified as a narcotic, one which some say supplies a dreamy escape. Thus the inspiration for their boat's name, we could assume."

"Creativity wasn't their strong point," Maximo said.

"No. Neither was choosing their battles. They happened to be the same guys who had given you an ultimatum about something," Bodkin said.

"Now I'm remembering. You helped out by sending our message for us. Messed with their boat a little."

"I didn't mess with it; I sunk it," Bodkin said.

"That's right. Yeah, I recall that. Nice. Much appreciated, Lee."

"Don't thank me, reward me."

"I'll have DiMarco call you back," Maximo said.

Sixteen minutes later, DiMarco called back.

Bodkin had never known the guy's first name. Didn't know, and didn't care.

"I have two such weapons, Mr. Bodkin. Duplicates actually. Had a shipment of five of them a year ago, and two have survived the year. I modified them a bit," DiMarco said.

"How so?" Bodkin said.

"Capacity. We upped it," DiMarco said.

"I love it," Bodkin said.

"Great. And each comes with a loaded magazine. Additional magazines are available for each gun at a nominal fee," DiMarco said.

"How many spare magazines you have?"

"At this time, four."

"Include all of them."

"But you haven't heard the pricing on them yet," DiMarco said.

"Throw them in free," Bodkin said.

"Uh, I'll have to talk to Geno and Maximo. I don't know," DiMarco said.

"I just talked to Maximo. Now is no time to get thrifty, DiMarco."

Silence.

"I sunk a yacht for you guys. Remember that?" Bodkin said.

"The extra magazines will be in the package," DiMarco said. "Expect it tomorrow by 8 AM. Some formidable folks up your way or something?"

"The folks are taken care of. We got some animal issues remaining, however," Bodkin said.

"You need this kind of setup for some wild animals? I thought you were a big hunter or whatever."

"You've not seen these particular critters."

"I think you're slipping, Mr. Bodkin," DiMarco said. The line went dead.

***

Official sunrise had arrived just 19 minutes earlier when the white Lincoln Town Car pulled into the hotel parking lot. Bodkin was outside, waiting.

A big, heavily built man, maybe 30 or so, stepped from the car. Dark eyes, dark hair, and sporting a small beard, no mustache. He wore a shiny black leather jacket; when he maneuvered from the Lincoln, Bodkin could see the shoulder holster underneath. Bodkin knew who he was from the past; a bad guy who did rough things. Mostly to other bad guys, but criminal behavior nevertheless. The man had picked up a long cardboard package from the floor on the passenger side before getting out; he handed the box to Bodkin.

Bodkin took the package, heavy with the pair of weapons tightly secured and protected inside of it.

"I'm Lenny," said the thug, extending his hand.

Bodkin ignored the hand. "Tell you what. If I need to address you, I'll just say 'hey.'"

"Sounds good. Mr. DiMarco says you're OK."

"That I am. Glad he thinks so," Bodkin said.

"Oh, he does. Wanted me to let you know, if matters get out of hand, he'd be glad to come up and straighten things out. He and a couple of his specialists."

Bodkin had to smile. "Trust me, DiMarco and his helpers are a force in an urban setting. Not here. The things we're hunting in those hills would see him as a steaming plate of old dago manicotti."

The thug started to say something else, then stopped speaking, looking back at Bodkin in surprise.

"Did you say 'dago'? I thought you were dating one of our people," said the thug.

"One of our people? What is this, the 15th century?" Bodkin said. "Anyway, thanks, you were quick." Bodkin handed him a neatly stacked fistful of 20s.

"Mr. DiMarco says we're already paid well, doesn't want us taking no tips," said the thug.

"You're refusing money? For the business you're in, that's considered shameful," Bodkin said.

The thug issued a half-grin, then clutched the money and stuffed it into his leather jacket. Bodkin nodded to him once, then turned and walked back to the hotel, hearing the sound of the big car accelerating out of the lot and back down Highway 61.

Yesterday, Gladdis had used her feminine wiles to secure the goods from the cannery. A box of fish remains. Bravo. And now the replacement weapons were here, and the ruse was about to be set in gear. Time to move out.

Fourteen

The wolf-dog bleated out a cry of longing, a whimpering series of needy moans. Suggesting more the anguish of a lost puppy than that of the adult dog – one full of guile and power – that it was. The cream-colored dog held its left back leg up off the snowy ground, displaying injury as it hobbled along. It went round and round in the bluff's clearing, its prints forming a crude semicircle in the snow.

At first, other than the sound of the dog's own yelps of suffering, the woods around it were quiet. A few minutes after the wounded dog's mournful sounds started to echo through the wilderness, the soft accompaniment of a lone songbird joined in. The chirping sound was that of a chickadee. The little bird's song, so ubiquitous across North America, was sung here year-round. Today its call drifted out in the forest like it did in so many other regions, its sounds signaling the absence of duress and the joys of nature. To other beasts, the call of its song signaled that a forest and the animals it contained were at ease. Everything was normal.

Chick-a-dee-dee.

Nine pairs of wolf ears listened to the chickadee song. Nine sets of wolf eyes watched the canine up the slope from them in its agony. A pleasant day with an ailing target. It was a perfect setting for one of their slaughters, followed by another blood feast. The wounded cream-colored dog was next on the menu.

The wolves were sure of their mission, as their quarry could do nothing but break into a full, struggling sprint and try to escape. It would be impossible for it to do so, however. Besides being wounded and outnumbered, this other animal had positioned itself near a precipice where there would be no escape. The further up the bluff, the narrower it became. Only a dense patch of brush lined one side of the rise, the side away from the river. Even if the dog burrowed itself in there, it wouldn't be a big challenge to rush into the thicket with its thorns and tangles, and then kill and wrench out the dog. They had the prey dead to rights, and the savoring of its body had already begun in their minds.

The dog had stopped whimpering, probably aware of the pack's approach. Trying to maintain a low profile, to hold still, but it was standing out in the open. No concealment, but it wouldn't have mattered anyway; it would be eaten regardless of what it did at this point. The outdoor surroundings were now silent, other than that single bird chirping its relaxed song.

Chick-a-dee-dee.

Then the bird's soft call changed ever so slightly, sounding off as a few brief chirps.

Chirp. Chirp. Chirp. Chirp.

The wolfpack in their eagerness never noticed the difference.

The dog, its back leg still lifted from the forest floor, limped into the dense brush, in the general direction of the bird's call. Probably seeking other animals that remained at ease, looking for some kind of pointless companionship in its last moments. The wolves marked the spot where the dog disappeared, and crept forward. Now leaving any of the narrow cover they'd hid in, stepping out onto open ground. To enhance the swiftness of the hunt.

Chick-a-dee-dee.

The issuance of the bird's call, now returning to its

normal cadence, assured them. Everything was normal, the slaughter could commence like usual.

Earlier, the wolves had been bedded down after a night's hunt and the killing and eating of two young deer fawns. Not enough, but better than nothing. They'd consumed an old man and his dog not long ago, and two younger males before that point. Teenagers, although the wolves couldn't grasp that concept. They simply thought of the two teenage boys as they did of the fawns they'd eaten: young, and excellent cuisine. After that, three more men with guns, who had come to hunt them. In turn, those men were also eaten by their group.

But too little volume for the whole pack of them, as numerous as they'd been at the time. They numbered fewer now, but other than the dark grey alpha wolf, the pack was hungry. As they'd consumed nearly every available animal in the area, food was becoming more and more sparse. Now down to people almost exclusively.

Then, late in the morning, the smell reached them as they'd rested in their beds in the thicket. Something foreign but alluring. A food source high in fat, but not a morsel which had ever been available to them before. The fragrance and promise was too much to resist. With the direction of the dark grey alpha, they were coaxed from the dense cover and left their bedding area to find out more.

Upon investigation, the morsels were easy to find, and the trail of them easy to follow. Protruding from tree branches overhead, the pieces of prey creatures rested, impaled, just above their line of sight. They could smell the spoiling skin, the brains, the eyes. Each wolf, including the alpha, had no experience with this type of food. But they wanted it. The alpha wouldn't let them, however; not yet. Just a little more exploration needed, then they could backtrack and devour the food source.

Salmon heads, from the cannery in downtown Taconite Bluff.

They'd been following the trail of posted fish heads, moving up the steep bluff, when the crippled dog appeared to them. As if in a dream. A dream of very good fortune, as their bellies were now empty and their mouths starting to salivate. If they'd had the power of deep reasoning, they'd almost have considered the cries of the injured dog to be a type of siren's song. Was caution required?

Chick-a-dee-dee.

If there'd been any danger, the bird would be the first to retreat. But it was still here. All was well. They'd now eat.

The wolfpack proceeded, moving in for the kill, led by the charcoal alpha wolf and a guardian wolf on either side of it. Its fangs were coated with an anticipatory froth and its amber eyes were alight. Time for savagery, time for fresh blood. And the alpha wolf stalked with supreme confidence, as it knew, in its primitive consciousness, that it was king of this forest. Reinforced from the time it was a puppy; it had always got what it needed, always overtook the other wolves in challenges. It controlled the other members of its pack, and they would always be there to protect it and serve it, until the end of time. The alpha wolf now reveled in the fact that it would eat first, while the others waited. As always. The beast assigned the title Product 68Q by its creators – who affectionately called it Red Fang – was the almighty apex predator. Of this forest, and of the world. It had been taught that, and in its remorseless reality, it knew it.

Alpha wolf mistake number one: The wolfen guardians it ran with would not guard it until the end of time; at this point, they actually would be guarding it for less than a minute.

Alpha wolf mistake number two: It was not the apex predator of the world; far from it. In actuality, right or wrong, only one creature on the planet currently occupied that spot. A creature poorly adapted for living in the wild, but one that thus created dwellings, machines, and coverings so it could survive almost anywhere. A creature nearly helpless when battling large wild predators, at least in its natural form. So this creature, *homo sapiens*, designed weapons so formidable it could practically destroy not just any other creature, but the world itself.

Other factors keeping *homo sapiens,* or humankind, on top were many, and beyond the grasp of beasts such as wolves. Memory, the use of tools, planning, and of course that special ability to create weapons. Oh yes, the weapons were disproportionately figured into the balance. The pack couldn't conceive of such things, and would thus learn them the hard way.

The wolves proceeded, closer to the brush near the top of the bluff. They positioned themselves out in the open, all the better to survey the vines, thorn bushes, and saplings, and to react quickly when their quarry burst into its final escape run. Then the charcoal-colored alpha wolf saw her looking back into its own eyes. The target prey, the injured blonde dog which had been crying out in helplessness moments ago, peered back at Product 68Q from the brush. The eyes and face of the other animal didn't show submission or defeat. In the unspoken visual communication between canines, the alpha wolf knew what it meant. Not fear, not the moment before flight. It was a view to a kill, the moment before a carnivorous conquest. The alpha's own favorite moment; now the alpha itself was the focus of it.

It was at that moment the big wolf learned one other

key ingredient in humankind's quiver of arrows, one that kept it at the peak of the totem pole on planet earth. A principle humankind executed over millennia with precision, in a way a wolf itself never could.

Humankind excelled at setting traps.

The instant the flashes and piercing bursts ignited, the wolves, every one of them, lowered their bodies in unison, in a panic, and took the first leaps to begin their escape. Tried to, at least.

A barrage of .30-caliber slugs, designed for war but capable of taking down elk eight times the size of each wolf, exploded from the darkness of the thicket and connected with canine ribs, shoulders, heads, and necks. Bodies whirled, recoiled, and collapsed, blood drops sprayed and specks of fur floated away in the icy winter breeze.

A massacre. The wolves had been lured into the open, and had nowhere to hide. From the first squeeze of a trigger to the time the pack sprawled dead or disabled on the snowy ground, just seven seconds had expired. Three wolves remained alive, wounded and struggling to escape.

Not for long. With the first gun reports still echoing through the hills, Lee Bodkin slipped between thorny branches to Sheba's right, Gladdis Montrose to her left, the stocky rifles in their hands now hot and leaking thin smoke streams. Bodkin approached the nearest canine, already with a bullet wound in its chest, disabling it and cutting life expectancy to another 25 seconds. The wolf whirled its massive head toward him, its mouth rearing back in a desperate and murderous snarl. Although mortally wounded, it started to rise up, trying to get to its feet. Bodkin shot it through the heart, dropping it, then shot it twice through the head, killing the wolf instantly. Montrose did the same to a separate animal nearby, three sharp pops dispatching the second wounded wolf. Bodkin looked up from his victim to spot the third and final predator.

"There's your boy!" Bodkin shouted to Montrose, stepping away from the dead wolf at his feet and looking down the slope. It was the charcoal alpha wolf, one rear leg dragging, crimson splashing into the snow from a pair of wounds behind its front shoulder. Hits to at least one lung, trauma that would have anchored any of the other wolves. But not Product 68Q, not yet.

Bodkin was ready to provide backup shots if needed, although the target was scurrying out of his own range of marksmanship effectiveness. But not beyond the range of Gladdis Montrose. It was her game. She got sure footing, then assumed a relaxed position, letting the iron sights of the semiautomatic rest on the rapidly moving but hobbled wolf. As Montrose took aim, Sheba, with her make-believe injured leg now miraculously healed, raced at top speed down the bluff to the alpha wolf. She caught up to it in seconds.

One hard nip into the big wolf's hind quarter made it stop and whirl, fangs bared. Facing the huge dark wolf, Sheba looked lightweight and small, like a skinny greyhound next to a muscular Rottweiler. Sheba lunged one step forward, then quickly back out of the giant's snapping range. Another lunge, another retreat. Playing out the strategy. The big charcoal wolf was forced to stay focused on the menacing dog.

Just as the alpha wolf had been taught to recognize a gun running empty, Sheba had learned the importance of a gun still loaded. And how to purposely act as a diversion, as a decoy. The maneater was focused on the dog, the dog's throat, anticipated the grip on the other animal, the act of killing it. Those thoughts and intentions were the last to enter its brain.

Bullets from the rifle Gladdis Montrose held struck the alpha's front leg, its rib cage, its neck, then its skull. Four shots, four hits. The big wolf collapsed in front of Sheba, air expelling from its now-dead jaws, steam drifting up and away into the frigid air. Blood recently nourished with the flesh of a mature man, his dog, two adventuresome teenagers, and three thugs flowed from the killer's body, painting the snow under it a bright red.

Bodkin and Montrose approached with rudimentary caution, but confident that the creature was now gone. Each of them held an M1A rifle, originally a military-issue design but recently produced on modern assembly lines. These two guns had been altered by a brutal but skillful weapons specialist in the cities far south from here; originally meant to hold magazines of 10 bullets, the guns had been altered to now hold supplies of 23 shells at a time. Bodkin had four or five shots left in his rifle, and Montrose now had two. Both of them removed the inserted magazines and fed in fresh ones, worked the slides so the guns were ready to shoot, and proceeded to the carcass.

Upon inspection it was confirmed: the urgent danger this pack had presented had now been nullified. Like his subjects, the alpha wolf was now dead.

The tail end of a predator call protruded from Lee Bodkin's pants pocket. The call was mainly used to bring in varmints like foxes and coyotes. It could be dialed to a pitch to mimic songbirds; he had the call currently set to chickadee. He stuffed the call deeper into his pocket, so it wouldn't be lost as they dragged the big, charcoal-colored wolf from the hills.

So much work left to do.

Fifteen

It was 7:55 AM. Bodkin knocked on Mickey Manoomin's back door – the door to his house, connected to the cafe his life revolved around. Three minutes later, Mickey answered. Bodkin stood there, his face pink, his eyes half closed. Under his left arm he held an elongated cardboard box.

"On Sundays I open at 10," Mickey said.

"I'll be out of town way before then. This won't take long," Bodkin said.

"I know it won't," Mickey said.

"I did bring a peace offering," Bodkin said. He lifted the cardboard package, and opened the top just enough to show Mickey the contents. Inside rested a shiny pair of glossy wooden limbs, the color of shiny maple syrup, tethered together with a jet-black bowstring. He closed the lid. "Yours to keep, if you promise to spread the word," Bodkin said.

"Hang on," Mickey said, and closed the house's door. Less than a minute later, the door to the cafe opened. Bodkin stepped in, and Mickey closed the door behind him, locking it.

"My first guess is espresso," Mickey said.

"Please," Bodkin said.

"Double?"

"Make it three."

"Tea as well?" Mickey said.

"You're a saint," Bodkin said.

"Flattery will get you nowhere," Mickey said.

Mickey scooped the coffee grounds, the chrome spoon clinking as it dumped Costa Rican bean powder into the espresso maker's receptacle. The device hissed and whirred, and the odor of the pungent brew drifted amongst the chairs and tables, their own aging wood smells blending with that of the hot liquid. The heat of the building had begun to envelope Bodkin's body, and his sleepy vision began to clear while his brain started to regenerate.

"You look wretched, Bodkin; you've got hours of driving ahead of you. Should I place a bet you wrap your truck around a tree heading back?"

"That would have been a possibility. But I won't be driving. Gladdis will; she's now getting some sleep. She says she hates the truck, but always drives it like she's in NASCAR. I predict a speeding ticket."

Mickey didn't reply, just leaned on the counter, looking down at it with still-sleepy eyes.

"Anyway. I came here to tell you about your canoe, and the padlock securing it; I've got some explaining to do," Bodkin said.

Mickey took the package resting near Bodkin's arm, the box containing hundreds of dollars worth of hunting bow, and set it on a lower shelf, on his own side of the counter. He turned and lifted the steaming tea kettle off the burner, poured the water into a mug and lowered a bag of ground mint leaves into it. Then he placed the hot tea in front of Bodkin, beside the half-empty espresso cup.

"Anybody ask ya?" Mickey said. He stepped lightly from around the counter and walked through the cafe to the door leading to his attached house. Bodkin heard the door open and close, the sounds barely above a whisper.

As he sat in the cafe, alone, Bodkin thought back to the events which had just played out. He'd heard his entire life that Lake Superior seldom gives up its dead. The truth of this legend is considered mystical, but the reason is scientific. Unusually frigid, the water of

Superior is consistently estimated at just about 36°F on average.

In normal lakes, with normal temps, bacteria will feed on a sunken dead body. This process will cause gas to form inside the body. As a consequence, the body will float to the surface after a matter of time. The water in Lake Superior is cold enough year-round to prevent this feeding by bacteria, and thus inhibit any floating bodies. They still disintegrate, but much slower, and stay down where they came to rest. On the bottom.

***

He and Gladdis had surveyed the dead wolves after the shooting bursts, then Bodkin proceeded with an examination of the biggest wolf's neck and shoulder area, digging his chilled fingers down into the still-warm fur, feeling along the muscle and bone underneath. Soon he found it: a radio frequency identification device, not much larger than a pea. There was no way this pseudo-federal gang was going to invest so much on a killer canine and not track it. Bodkin knew where most RFID chips were located on dogs: under the loose skin of the shoulders. It's the most accessible area on a beast and causes the least interference. He was familiar with the procedure – he'd had one implanted in Sheba.

Wirth had given it away more than once on their hike to find the big wolf's lair: he knew its general location already. They'd even brought Bodkin to a spot on the edge of the forest which led most directly to it. But, Bodkin concluded, Wirth knew its area, but had no idea how to hunt it, how to ambush it. That's why he needed to see the lair's location from a distance, and see how he could maneuver toward it. Let Bodkin help them set up a surprise attack on the big wolf. Of course, the opposite had occurred: while planning a surprise attack, he and his thugs were the ones who'd been ambushed. Poetic justice.

Bodkin dug the chip out from the wolf's body with his knife, placed it on a boulder, and smashed it with another heavy stone. Red Fang's location could only be determined in an old-school way now, no more satellite intelligence. Making that impossible was next on their agenda.

After two hours of dragging the heavy carcass from the tree-covered hills, they'd stowed it by the roadside, in the brush. After dark, they took the truck down the highway to where the carcass was hidden, and after wrapping the carcass in a canvas tarp, heaved it into the truck bed. Then they secured another tarp over the bed to conceal it, and drove back to the hotel, the big wolf now in their possession.

Gladdis cocooned in her room to grab as much sleep as possible; for the journey home, she'd be the driver. Bodkin set his Swiss watch for three hours of sleep. Had to be back out before sunrise. He was.

It's easier to apologize than to get permission. Bodkin had known that for years, and acted accordingly. With his rig waiting on a frontage road 400 yards down the shore, Bodkin stalked in silence into Mickey's backyard. Didn't want to do the next thing he'd planned, but saw little other choice. The wolf's body couldn't be just discarded anywhere. It had to rest in a spot no one would find it. Where nobody, no group, could use its DNA to replicate it. To create the monstrosity again and again.

A communiqué with Lita via phone last night suggested some federal agents, "researchers" they called themselves, were coming to this fine region to recover their work. One Major Wirth no longer responded to their need for updates, and they were concerned. They'd be coming for Product 68Q, specifically for its DNA. Couldn't have that.

Burn it? The problem with that, as far as he knew, was that carbon residue might still provide enough DNA to reuse. Best to not have the beast found at all. And time was running out.

So Mickey's canoe got its first test run. In the dark, Bodkin used his skinning knife to pick – and destroy – the lock securing the heavy chain of the birchbark canoe. Bodkin found an old paddle in the ancient woodshed of the yard. A second lock jimmied and ruined. Bodkin would be owing some favors. After that, it was easy to drag the canoe to the shore section near his truck's parking spot, with the birchbark material being as light as it was.

The heavy carcass of a killer wolf was then loaded into the canoe, the canvas still wrapped around it. After two volleyball-sized rocks were stuffed into the tarp next to the body, and the tarp secured back in place again, the package was ready for a watery grave.

Navigating the icy waters in the handcrafted canoe was easier than expected, with the weight of the dead load stabilizing the front of the vessel. Familiar with the depths from many past fishing attempts, Bodkin paddled out to where the bottom dropped from 30 feet to 60 feet, then suddenly to over 100 feet. There, with some careful effort, a lot of balancing against big waves rocking the vessel, and one big splash, he plunked the body of Product 68Q – aka Red Fang – over the front of the canoe, where it twirled to the bottom of a frigid and forbidding body of water. Just over 100 feet down, the carcass rested and awaited its inevitable decay. Never to be recovered.

***

Earlier, just as the sun came up, the canoe returned to shore. The big lake had swallowed up the charcoal wolf, but not Bodkin. He was now back indoors in the warmth, safe for the moment. With exhaustion quaking through his body, he listened to the creaking of the old building as the breeze from Lake Superior stroked it. Then Bodkin sipped the scalding hot tea, letting the steam wash over his nose and cheeks, melting away a little of Superior's chill.

###

P. J. Hafner is a St. Paul, Minnesota, native. Both an angler and bow hunter, he also spent 15 years as a wrestler and judo fighter, and is a repeat participant in the Twin Cities marathon and other running races. He's hiked in the Blue Ridge, Cascade, Chuckanut and Rocky Mountains, as well as in Switzerland and Iceland. Hafner holds degrees in English and Kinesiology.

He is also the author of *Stalk*, *Chuckanut Stalk*, and *Marathon Stalk*.

www.ingramcontent.com/pod-product-compliance
Lightning Source LLC
Chambersburg PA
CBHW051507170626
46811CB00002B/687